DEAD MAN'S COVE

Published in Canada by Engen Books, St. John's, NL.

Library and Archives Canada Cataloguing data is available on the publisher's website.

ISBN-13: 978-1-77478-198-2

Distributed by:
Engen Books
www.engenbooks.com
submissions@engenbooks.com

First mass market paperback printing: September 2025

Cover Image: Engen Books

DEAD MAN'S COVE

KIM DURNFORD-COURTNEY

ENGEN
BOOKS

Dedicated to my husbandCharles, the person who loves me for exactly who I am and the one who has always encouraged me to "just do it ."

And to my two daughters, Lexi and Sarah, who are my greatest achievements in life.

PROLOGUE
1943

The room smelled of death: a heavy, nauseous stench that permeated the air and thickened itself as it forced its way inside your nostrils.

The putrid green blinds were pulled completely over the windows to hinder any form of life on the outside from entering the deathly cavity. Yet, nature being the supreme being, life still insisted upon its presence being acknowledged, and would not be refused. Brilliant bursts of lightning forced their way through the hideous window coverings without apology. Continuous eruptions of resounding thunder shook the dwellings' aged and dilapidated foundation to its very core. It howled and raged, seething with anger like unrequited grief.

Inside the abode, even death would not hold back secrets from being whispered. Like death, with all its mystery, thus were the final words spilt from parched lips of a clandestine soul.

In time, as with death, all became silent.

It was then she came...

CHAPTER ONE
1903

After the foggy days of July, Naomi was delighted to bask in the heat of the blazing sun under a cloudless azure sky that came with the turn of a calendar page. As Levi rowed his small blue dory across the sparkling waters of Cape La Hune Bay, Naomi was content just to sit and take in the beauty of the rugged landscape that surrounded her. Queen, the couple's old, shaggy brown dog and Naomi's constant companion, stood at the ready with her paws on the gunnel as she surveyed what was going on around her. Tail wagging and tongue panting anxiously, Queen stood eagerly, anticipating all the new smells and delights that this trip was about to offer her.

"What a beautiful day. Perfect for berry picking," Levi stated, breaking the silence. His oars cut into the calm waters creating the only ripples to be seen on the surface of the bay.

"Yes," Naomi answered, as she emerged from her relaxed trance. "I hope the berries are ripe and plentiful this year."

She hoped to line the shelves of her cellar with as

many jars of blueberries as she could. The sweet sapphire berries would be added to the many jars of the tart, amber-coloured bake-apples she had finished bottling a week ago. These staples would be a fine start to the provisions that would see them through the desolate winter months when such luxuries could not be obtained elsewhere.

"It looked like there were going to be a good many berries when I was over here a few weeks ago. We didn't get any lightning to dry up the flowers this spring so the blossoms should be okay," Levi said.

"Well, if we could get enough, I would put away a few bottles to give to Ruth. Having had her baby the night before last, she won't be doing much berry picking yet for a while. With eleven other children besides baby Thomas, she'll have enough to keep her busy."

Naomi's youngest sister Ruth lived next door to her, and although her nieces and nephews were like her own children, Naomi had not been blessed with babies of her own. Even though her house was seldom empty of children and there was always one or more at her table during mealtime, Naomi still yearned for a baby of her own. Fate though, had so far been a cruel master and Naomi and Levi had never had their prayers answered.

"I'm sure Ruth would love to have you do some bottling for her. It would be a great help to her and Luke for the winter. I guess Luke got his wish too. He told me the other day that if Ruth could have one more boy, he'd have enough to fit out his own schooner." Levi laughed. "He said with the seven boys he has now, and then if he got one more, he would have a fine crew. I guess little Thomas did it for him," he chuckled.

"I think it will be a few years yet before Thomas will be working aboard a schooner." Naomi grinned. "But Luke has a fine bunch of young men growing up around him."

"Yes, he certainly does, and I am pretty thankful for all the work they do for me too. I cannot remember the last time I've had to chop or split any wood. Young Cecil is almost a permanent fixture out by my woodpile. I can tell you that it's a big load off me." Levi paused and sighed pensively. "Yes sir, Luke has a good bunch of young men to be sure."

As Naomi turned her head toward the sea and sighed as well, nothing more was spoken of children. It was an ache they both felt and an unfulfilled wish they each had been left with.

As Levi and Naomi drifted comfortably into their own private thoughts, the oars of the tiny dory were pushing them closer and closer to their ultimate destination: Dead Man's Cove.

Dead Man's Cove was a low valley that had no harbour to speak of. It consisted only of a shoreline of flat rocks where a boat could very easily be hauled onto the shore. It was well situated within Cape La Hune Bay, and was trumped by towering hills on the end of the cove leading further into the large fiord. There were no trees, and the valley was covered with berry bushes and low shrubs. The proximity to the settlement of Cape La Hune made it the ideal spot to pick berries and was where Naomi and Levi usually went to fill their buckets on their annual berry picking trip. It was also the ideal spot for old dogs like Queen to have a playful romp and eke out any hidden tastes and smells that the place was hiding.

Levi headed the dory to a flat spot on the shoreline and jumped over the gunnel. As quick as Levi was getting ashore, old Queen was quicker. She was out of the small boat and rolling in the brambles and tucks before Levi's feet hit the rocks. Levi took the bow line and easily pulled the small dory onto the flat rocks of the shore. He then tied the line to a large, bleached driftwood log that was jammed between some rocks above the highwater mark. The flat surface of the shoreline made it easy for Naomi to step ashore.

"Be careful not to slip on the rocks; sometimes the kelp can make them slippery," Levi cautioned, as he held Naomi's hand to help her out of the boat.

"You would think I couldn't get out of a dory on my own." His sure-footed wife laughed. In an instant, Levi grabbed her from the edge of the dory and swung her around, causing Naomi to squeal.

"You, my darling, are the best thing I have, and I only want to keep you safe!" And with that Levi firmly kissed her on the lips.

Realizing they may be seen by others across the bay, Naomi gently but regrettably eased herself away from the kiss. "If anyone sees us, they'll think we came here for more than berry picking," she laughed playfully and lovingly smoothed her hand down the rough cheek of the man who held her heart.

"Whatever you wish, my dear." Levi grinned, totally amused by the slow stain of red that was colouring his wife's cheeks.

"Levi Spencer! Are you going crazy today? I am here to go berry picking!" With a quick turn of her back, Naomi, feigning disbelief, headed along the shoreline with her bucket in her hand, leaving a grinning Levi to find his own berry patch. Old Queen, looking as perplexed as it were possible for a dog to look, headed after her mistress and was soon caught up in fluttering butterflies and curious smells.

The morning's show of affection had Naomi wearing a smile all day. As she and Queen slowly picked their way along the perimeter of Dead Man's Cove, Naomi saw Levi on the far side of the valley edging his way behind a small knoll as he picked. She knew she was a lucky woman to have found a man as loving as her husband. If only their love had given them children as well. With a small sigh and a whisper of, "Maybe someday," Naomi bent her head and continued to fill her bucket from a large patch of berries she had found.

Totally preoccupied with all the fruit hanging rich and ripe from the bushes, Naomi rose suddenly when a low mournful cry reached her ears. Listening closely, the sound once more caught her attention. As she took a quick glance around the surrounding area, Naomi realized that Queen, whom she thought was right beside her, was nowhere to be seen. Thinking it may have been the old dog making the frightful sound, Naomi called to the animal.

"Queen! Queen! Where are you, girl?"

Expecting the dog to come bounding through the bushes as usual, Naomi was surprised to not have received a sudden appearance from her constant companion. Instead, her answer came as a loud, whining cry, as if someone were hurt or sick. Naomi's first thought was that Queen had fallen and injured herself. Naomi rushed toward the pitiful moan that seemed to be coming from below the ridge she was standing on. Scrambling clumsily down a steep rocky incline, Naomi saw Queen laying flat on her stomach beneath the stony outcropping. The dog was looking straight ahead at a small opening in the rocks and a low whine, as if something there was hurting her, was the only sound she made.

Kneeling beside Queen, Naomi gently smoothed the dog's head with her hand.

"What's the matter, Queen? What is it, girl?" Naomi questioned the animal. Visually she could see nothing that was causing the dog any pain, but Queen lay motionless as she stared at the opening and whimpered pitifully.

"Is there something in there, Queen?" Naomi knew if the dog had seen a small animal in the cave, she would not be lying still. Rather the poor little creature would be on the run with the old dog in hot pursuit.

Curiosity was getting the better of Naomi and whatever was causing Queen to be in this mournful state was worth trying to figure out. Standing and looking toward the other side of the valley where she had last seen Levi, Naomi realized he was no longer in her sight. She would have much rather her husband go into the cave for a look but seeing as how he was nowhere to be seen, Naomi decided she would check things out herself so as not to keep her beloved animal in such an agonizing state. Reaching down, Naomi lovingly patted Queen's shaggy brown head.

"I can't see Levi anywhere, Queen, so I guess I'll have to take a look and see what has upset you so much."

For the first time since Naomi had arrived at the dog's

side, Queen raised her head off the ground and looked directly at her mistress. Naomi felt a shudder run the length of her spine. Queen had a haggard appearance and what she could have sworn were tears on the silky fur beneath her soulful, brown eyes. She whined pitifully at Naomi before turning away to face the entrance of the cave once again.

As she stood alongside her cherished friend and stared at the cave's small opening, Naomi's body trembled. Something was compelling Naomi toward the opening. She knew with a profound certainty that she had to go inside. Squeezing between the two boulders that created the narrow opening, the sunlight immediately died and like a lamplight that had suddenly been extinguished, a thick darkness covered Naomi. She blinked her eyes repeatedly as she tried to focus her eyesight from the bright sunlight to the semi-darkness that seemed to smother the interior of the chamber. A musty, dank smell stuck to her nostrils as it hung thick in the stale, damp air. As Naomi's sight adjusted to her surroundings, she started to feel confined. The cave was underneath the ridge she had been previously berry picking on and although it was not large, it was quite high enough to stand straight inside. Trying to focus on the tight enclosure, a macabre chill penetrated the air, causing Naomi to shiver uncontrollably. Noticing what looked like a flat rocky ledge toward the back of the cave, Naomi grabbed the edge as she sat herself down. The ledge was covered with spruce boughs and branches that were greyed and bare with age. Naomi immediately felt herself getting dizzy as the air seemed to be thick and hard to breathe. Wrapping her arms about herself for urgent warmth and to control the incessant shivering she was overcome with, Naomi knew she should get out of the cave, but her mind was reeling. All she wanted was to sleep. To close her eyes and rest.

At that moment and without warning, a feeling of warmth, like a quilt in the blazing sun, melted through Naomi's body. Laying down on the brittle tree branches as if they were a cozy feather mattress, she felt the anxiety and cold leaving her body and sleep like a shield blocking her thoughts from the world around her. In the far distance, Naomi became faintly aware of the sound of someone singing. Her eyes were too heavy to open, but the soulful melody would not let her completely give in to the sleep she so desperately wanted. Repeatedly, the melodic voice kept pulling her back from total bliss. Suddenly, as if she had been doused with a bucket of cold water, Naomi jolted awake. Trying to make sense of her surroundings, she felt the sharpness of the spiny boughs as they stabbed into her neck and back. The blackness of the rocky ceiling above her head brought her to her senses. As she shoved her way off the stone ledge, Naomi turned and found herself staring into the deep white hallows of a human skull.

At that very instant, Levi heard a scream that filled the very air around him, while Queen eerily howled like a wolf on a night of a full moon.

***

Racing toward where he had just heard the terrifying sounds, Levi found Naomi laying on the ground outside the cave. Queen was lying beside her, protectively nuzzling his mistress' hand. Shaking her gently, Naomi awoke as if she had been peacefully sleeping in her own bed. As Levi described his frightening ordeal, Naomi seemed totally unaware of anything that had taken place. Quickly, but tenderly, Levi led his wife back to the boat and settled her in place. He pulled the oars with all his strength, knowing in his own mind, he could not get home soon enough to try to forget the whole experience that had him totally unnerved. With no way to explain what had taken place in Dead Man's Cove, Levi was completely mystified.

Naomi, sitting on the taut, her back to Levi and with old Queen licking her hand, could do nothing but smile.

CHAPTER TWO
1943

Morgan Spencer bailed water from his flat-bottom dory when the sudden darkening of the sky caused him to stop what he was doing and look up. Glancing at the entrance to the harbour, the southern horizon looked black and ominous. A maelstrom of towering clouds billowed heavenward in what looked to transform into an early spring tempest, wild with wind and rain.

Morgan began moving a bit faster, to complete his work before the storm hit the tiny community of Cape La Hune. His final task was to check his moorings to ensure they were secure against the impending gale. Once satisfied that all was fastened and holding firm, Morgan climbed the railings, toggled the stage door and headed up the gravel pathway toward home. A home where his mother lay dying.

Morgan Levi Spencer, an affirmed bachelor who lived his forty-one years with his parents, was sure that he would soon be living alone.

His father, Levi Spencer, had died peacefully in his sleep three years ago. At eighty-three years, Levi often said that his was a life well lived. Now his mother, Naomi, lay dying in the same bed as his father, and Morgan knew her well-lived life was soon to come to an end as well. A sudden stroke about a week ago had rendered her unable to either move or utter a word since it had happened.

As Morgan approached the house, he saw his Aunt Ruth by the gate door and his other aunt, Kitty Pink waddling her over-burdened frame down the opposite path toward her home. Kitty Pink, or Aunt Kitty as she was respectfully known, was the community mid-wife, as well as the official nurse in Cape La Hune. Getting on in age, Aunt Kitty possibly had a hand in every birth and death for the last sixty years. She had also mended more cuts, burns, scrapes, and pulled more teeth than Morgan could count, including his own. Even though she found it hard getting around these days, she made sure to see her oldest sister, Naomi, every day, though there was nothing she could do.

Ruth Barter, Naomi's youngest sister, spent every spare minute she could by her bedside. They had lived next door to each other for the past sixty-three years and had helped raise each other's family. The significant difference being that Ruth had an overly impressive brood of fourteen children, whereas Naomi remained childless until the age of forty-two when her one and only child, Morgan, was born.

A baby born on the change, was how Aunt Kitty and the other harbour women described it. The only change, as far as Naomi knew, was the joy that her son brought to her life. Morgan was Naomi's greatest love as well as her best kept secret.

***

"My boy, you look too tired to even fall down," Aunt Ruth said as she swung open the gate door to let Morgan into the yard. "I have a dipper of stewed fish on the tail end of the stove keeping warm for you. There is also a fresh bun of bread on the counter, in the pantry."

"You are a God-sent Aunt Ruth," Morgan replied as he made his way up the walk to the porch door. "I don't know what I would do without you." Morgan walked around to the wood pile at the corner of the house and grabbed an armful of the stacked logs. "I'll take a bit in now and get some more after supper. Hopefully before the rain comes," he murmured to himself, with a nod to the threatening sky.

"The wood box is already full and so is the water barrel," Aunt Ruth said, indicating the large wood cask by the porch door. "Peter and Daniel came over about an hour ago and filled everything for you. With the bad weather coming, we figured you wouldn't get time before you finished salting down your fish in the stage."

"Those two boys are wonderful workers that Naomi Jane and Gilbert have there," Morgan smiled, referring to Aunt Ruth's daughter and son-in-law and their two sons. "Tell both of the boys I'll take them out in the boat with me the next chance I get."

"I'll tell them when I go in the house. Since Uncle Luke died and Naomi Jane and Gilbert moved in with me, they have taken a big burden off my shoulders, I can tell you."

Morgan glanced at the upstairs window above the porch door and with no reference needed asked, "How is she?"

"The same thing, my son. I think I saw her eyes flicker once but other than that, nothing." Aunt Ruth released a heavy sigh before continuing, "I've talked to her and said every prayer I know but not a sound or motion. All I am sure of is that she can't stay like that much longer." Aunt Ruth wiped her eyes in the tail of her flour sack apron.

"Well, you should go home now and lay down for a bit. This is hard on you too and Mam wouldn't want you getting yourself down because of her. I'll stay up with her tonight. That storm is getting pretty close, and I don't think you should be out in this kind of weather," Morgan voiced in concern.

"Oh, Gilbert told me to tell you that he was going to lay down for a couple of hours after supper and then he would come over and stay with Naomi for you to get some sleep."

"Tell Gilbert I said that would be wonderful. Now go over and get some rest yourself. The Lord only knows what we will have facing us tomorrow."

Aunt Ruth turned and headed across the yard toward her own white limed two-storey house. "Make sure you eat that stewed fish I brought over and don't forget the bun of bread in the pantry," she called over her shoulder as she reached for the latch on the porch door.

Morgan held up his hand in acknowledgement as he too reached for the string on the door latch. The storm was starting to show itself and with one arm filled with wood, the door nearly blew out of his hand from the sudden gust of wind.

As he barred the door to keep the fury outside, Morgan realized the big kitchen seemed a bit chilly as he entered the interior. Taking a few of the pieces of wood he had brought in, he added them to the red, hot cinders at the bottom of the stove. The dry birch started to pop and crackle almost as soon as Morgan had put the cover back on the old wood stove taking some small bits of peace the heat would soon fill the house.

He lifted the cover off the pot that Aunt Ruth had left on the stove for him. Inside was a stew of cod fish and potatoes in a warm broth. The smell was heavenly, but Morgan put the cover back on the pot, deciding he would eat it after he had checked on his mother.

Climbing the narrow stairway that led to the bedrooms on the second storey, the creaks and cracks of the painted wood stairs were as familiar as an old friend. Growing up in the house as a child, Morgan learned which treads to step over and how to precisely put your foot so as to avoid being detected when sneaking down the stairs. Many a night he would sneak out of his bed and expertly traverse his way to the lower level so he could listen when his parents had company visit their home. Almost as many times, Morgan must have fallen asleep at the bottom of those same stairs because when dawn broke the sky the next morning, he would find himself back and tucked into his own bed for the second time that night. He never got in trouble for his mischievousness, and knew it was always loving arms that carried him back up over those old stairs.

Heading down the hallway toward his mother's room, Morgan heard the shrieking howl of the wind as it pitched on the land. Rain hit like fingernails on the windowpane at the end of the hallway. Although it was not yet night, the sky had grown dark and broody, causing its cover to be spread over the community earlier than usual. "I got home just in time," Morgan said aloud to no one in particular.

Upon entering his mother's room, Morgan felt like he was going into a cave. The dark green blind covered the window, restricting any light from entering. The small kerosene lamp on the nightstand by the bed was turned to a low flicker and the room was cast in unnatural shadows. Morgan felt as if he were stifling. He quickly moved to the window where he yanked on the blind, raising it and letting in what daylight was left. "There's no need for us to be in the dark yet, is there, Mam?" Morgan spoke to his mother as if she were going to answer him but guessing she would not. "You always did sit and watch the storms through the window. You can lay there tonight, and I'll keep watch over everything for you," he reassuringly told her, wishing she would give some sign that she even knew he was there.

She looked so peaceful laying there as if she were sleeping. Her silver hair flowed over her shoulders and seemed to shine against the snow-white pillowcase where her head gently rested. It seemed as if she had taken on a more youthful appearance over the last few days. The former creases and lines of age and angst seemed to have smoothed away like the ripples in a pond. Morgan sincerely prayed that the look of contentment he saw meant his mother was without pain and at peace with her well-lived life.

Since she had taken ill, Naomi's favourite rocking

chair had been brought in from the kitchen and placed at the head of the bed. It served as a comfortable seat for the many family and friends who came to keep vigil by her side. Sitting himself down on the cushioned seat, Morgan was flooded with memories of the many times his mother rocked him in this very chair. He could feel her arms wrapped snugly and protectively around him, holding him as if she would never let him go. Growing up, Morgan knew he was loved but oftentimes his mother's over-protective nature was a bone of contention between them. His mother would have rather kept him constantly by her side while Morgan wanted to run, play, climb the hills, fish from the wharves, and just get into the typical mischief that other boys his age were getting into. Morgan's father, Levi, often had to speak up against rules that Naomi had laid down for their son. He was constantly trying to reassure her that there was no need for the protectiveness that Naomi constantly tried to bind Morgan with. It seemed to Morgan that his safety and welfare was what caused the most tension between his parents and so, oftentimes he would just let his mother have her way as he stayed close to home. It was easier doing this, than to see the worry on her face. In later years, when Morgan was old enough to court the young ladies of Cape La Hune, his mother always had some reason why he should not be seeing one or another. In this matter she was adamant, and Levi could not stop her from voicing her opinion on why the women were not good enough for their son. "Maybe one day a nice girl will visit that will be more suited to you," was an often-heard reason Morgan got from his mother. Yet, as the years passed, there was never any visitor that showed the attributes that it seemed Naomi thought worthy of her son's affection. Thus, he remained a man without a wife.

Morgan sometimes wondered what it would be like to have a family but, after all these years, it was not something that he took too much time to consider. Life was what you made of it and with fishing, taking care of the house and his aged parents, living day by day was enough to consider so Morgan never gave too much thought to his future.

As he muddled through the memories and thoughts that were invading his mind, Morgan's body, tired after a long day of work, soon settled into the comfort of the old rocking chair and slumber covered him like a heavy, warm blanket. But, somewhere between the world of sleep and wakefulness was a threshold that Morgan felt himself standing on — a threshold he was not sure if he should cross. On one side he could see his mother laying in the bed and on the other was an opening to a cave. The pull toward the cave was overpowering and he felt as if it were something he was compelled to do. Glancing back toward his mother, he saw her blue eyes gently opening as she looked directly at her son and softly whispered, "She is calling you. You must go." As he placed his foot over the threshold of the cave, Morgan knew his life would never be the same again.

***

That one step forward transported Morgan to the centre of a small, musty cave that was dank and eerily uncomfortable. The interior was dark, and Morgan squinted his eyes as he tried to see. At that instant, a pure white light poured down from the ceiling and shone directly on the back wall of the cave. Its luminous glow was so intense, Morgan rose his hands to shield his eyes, while its warmth compelled him to advance forward. Little by little he approached a protruding ledge at the back of the cave where the vivid brilliance of the light illuminated the bleached, white bones of a human skeleton like something being presented to him.

Rather than feeling horror or fear, Morgan felt a sudden melancholy and a desperate need to protect the exposed remains. As if it were a body that was stripped naked and deliberately exploited, Morgan took the dried limbs and twigs and tried to cover its bareness. It was then that his eyes fell on a set of tiny, white bones that were nestled within the body of the adult. He now understood that what was in front of him was a woman who had either been with child or the baby died laying on her chest. The delicate bones of her baby were now enclosed within that of its mother. Tears fell from Morgan's eyes and landed on the fragile bones of the child. He felt a love so pure and genuine for this tiny human, he was overcome with emotion. Reaching down within the chest of the woman, Morgan laid his hand on the delicate skull of the infant. Like a flash, he found himself standing in the cave holding a tiny newborn baby in his arms — a baby he knew was his. Morgan was amazed by a feeling of love and peace that he had never in his life felt before. He held what he knew was pure innocence within the shelter of his arms. As he turned to face the shelf where the remains of the woman were, a blood-curdling scream rent the air and seemed to fill the whole room and everything around him.

As if hit with a splash of cold water, Morgan bolted awake and grabbing the arms of the old rocking chair, was about to rise from the seat when a brilliant flash of lightning filled the room with such intensity that the electricity could be felt tingling, like a shiver, over his skin. At that same instant, Naomi rose from her pillow that had been her dying place for the last week. Her rheumy, blue eyes looked directly into the deeper blue eyes of her beloved son, and she softly whispered, "She is coming." Startled by the actions of his dying mother, Morgan could do nothing but stare at her, knowing only moments before his mother had been unable to move or speak. "She is coming. Love her, my son. Love her," Naomi's voice pleaded as the tears poured down her aged cheeks.

"Who is coming, Mam?" Morgan pleaded, grabbing his mother's gnarled hand. But without answer, Naomi peacefully lay back on her pillow, closed her eyes, and took her last breath.

CHAPTER THREE

Feeling as if his mind was disoriented, Morgan stood by his bedroom window and gazed out at the vibrancy of the full moon as it shone brightly over the windless harbour. His thoughts whirled in his head like a leaf being blown around in a hurricane. Sleep refused to let him close his eyes even though his body begged and pleaded for rest.

It had been nearly two weeks since his mother had passed, and he had barely slept a wink since then. The first three days after his mother's passing were a constant blur of people coming and going through his house as he tried to set everything in order for the wake and the funeral itself. Then came the agony of saying goodbye as they laid his mother within the muddy earth.

Since then, the silence within the walls of his home was deafening as he went from a constant throng to being by himself and noiselessly walking the memory-filled rooms alone. Although Morgan was fine with the quiet and being alone, since the night his mother passed away, his mind had been in a constant turmoil. He could not get the dream from that fateful night out of his head — if it had even been a dream.

Morgan could still feel the infant in his arms, could still feel its insubstantial weight and feel its silky skin against his own. He could picture every feature of the child's face and the silky black hair that covered its head. Even the smell of innocence that covered the infant lingered in his nostrils. The dankness and stagnant odour of the cave's interior permeated his senses, as did on the feeling of the rocky floor on the soles of his feet. Morgan's mind kept taking him back to the scene that played out before him that unforgettable night when his whole world changed forever. How could something that felt so real be just a dream?

Shaking his muddled head to try and clear his thoughts, Morgan pulled on his pants, took the kerosene lamp that was always kept lit in the hallway and headed to the kitchen to make himself a cup of tea. The clock above the stove showed that it was five minutes until midnight. If he could get a good, strong cup of tea, he may settle his mind enough to get a few hours of sleep before it was time to rise and go fishing.

Checking the kettle and finding that it was nearly empty, Morgan headed to the porch where the water buckets were kept filled. Taking a small dipper from the nearby table, he proceeded to fill the kettle then turned to head back to the kitchen. The full moon was casting its vivid brilliance on the ground outside and as he passed the porch window, Morgan was astonished to see a woman standing totally naked in the yard. The moonlight was illuminating her every curve as she held her arms in the air as if trying to touch the moon itself. Her hair, black as a raven's wing, hung down to her waist and swung to and fro as her body flowed in a rhythmic dance. Astonishingly mesmerized by the young woman's actions, Morgan could do nothing but stand and watch as she twirled around the garden under the lunar glow. Her movements mimicked music as she undulated to a silent melody that seemed to permeate the very air as her body swayed. The image was beyond anything his eyes had ever seen before, and her beauty held him in captivated fascination.

So intrigued was he, by the scene before him, Morgan's relaxed hand let slip the cover for the kettle he was holding. The clatter of metal on the wood floor broke the silence of the night, as the woman stood as still as a statue in the middle of the gravel pathway.

"Damn!" Morgan reached for the latch on the door, praying he did not frighten the woman away. To his surprise, as he stepped through the doorway and onto the bridge, she was moving toward him. Neither trying to cover her nakedness or seeming ashamed of it, her beauty cast an aura that was almost ethereal.

Standing a mere arm length from Morgan, he could see that her deep-set eyes were as black as the night sky. A small section of her silken hair hung down and covered the tan-colored skin of her delicate breast. High cheekbones framed a slender face that too was deeply tanned, both from the sun, as well as from indigenous roots that were prominently featured, a fact that aroused his sense of curiosity all the more.

Seeming to study Morgan as well, the woman gave him a subtle smile as she stepped past him and walked through the porch door and into the house.

Following along behind her, as if he himself were the stranger, Morgan stood at the porch door watching her as she surveyed the interior of the room. She seemed enthralled by the concept of the simplistic kitchen as she rubbed her hands along the walls and furniture. Reaching toward the kerosene lantern on the counter, like a moth to a flame, the heat expelled soon caused her to withdraw her hand again. Moving to the table, she lifted one end of the snow-white flour sack cloth that covered it. She moved her fingers along the delicately embroidered edges that had been sewn by his mother. Removing the cloth and touching it to her face, as if it were the most expensive silk, she expertly wrapped the fabric over one shoulder and around her body. Spying a piece of line that was by the wood box she tied it around her waist to form a belt for what became a unique dress. Rubbing her hand over the tail of the dress, she smiled as she gave a twirl in the middle of the kitchen floor.

Still watching the unbelievable scene that was playing out before him, Morgan continued his observation of the woman as he stood in total astonishment. The crackle of the burning wood from the stove caught her attention as she moved toward the source of the heat. Standing there for a moment, she then lowered herself to the bare floor and crossed her legs in front of the old iron stove as she extended her hands to take in the radiating warmth.

Walking slowly across the kitchen, Morgan took one of the chairs from the table and sat down next to her. Tilting her head and staring up into his face with a look of confusion, she patted the floor next to her in invitation and smiled. Feeling as if he were lording over her, Morgan got up, pushed the chair aside, and crossing his legs, he sat next to her on the hard kitchen floor, a place he hadn't been since he played there as a child. Yet tonight it somehow felt right.

Morgan could not take his eyes off the unusual stranger sitting next to him. She sat straight and proud as her long, nimble fingers combed through a strand of her thick, black hair. As he watched in fascination, she began to braid her hair together, separating it into three pieces before she started intertwining the silky locks. The act was hypnotizing as her fingers worked the rope of hair down one side of the flowing mane. Upon reaching the final twist, she took a strand of the rope belt from her waist and tied it tightly, holding the neatly woven braid secure.

Without thinking, Morgan reached forward and ran his fingers down the length of the silken braid. As each of them turned toward the other, blue eyes met black in a union of understanding. Morgan saw a calmness within her and a strength that surprised him. He knew there would be so much he would learn from her and so much he wanted to know. Like reacting to a lover, the woman lifted her hand and smoothed it over his rough, whiskered cheek as her thumb traced the outline of his lips.

"You are her."

She nodded and laid her head in his lap.

CHAPTER FOUR

"An Indian woman? Where did she come from?" Aunt Ruth asked as her jaw dropped in sheer disbelief.

"I... don't know. She just showed up in the yard last night. I don't know who she is or where she came from," Morgan uttered, intentionally leaving out the fact that she had been dancing naked in the moonlight and not wanting to have his aunt in hysterics at this bit of sordid information. He felt he was giving her more than enough now to chew on by even telling her about this unusual stranger.

'Well, what is her name? What is she doing over at your mother's house?"

"She hasn't spoken a word since she arrived. I don't know what to tell you, Aunt Ruth, other than that she is at the house, covered up in a blanket that I put over her so she wouldn't get cold while lying on the floor by the wood stove," Morgan rattled on in a string of his own disbelief of what he was actually saying. He was as flabbergasted as his Aunt Ruth, whose face had gone pale at the image her nephew was painting in her muddled head.

Morgan's mind was spinning like a whirlwind trying to make sense of what he was trying to tell another person. "Will you come over to the house with me and see for yourself? Maybe she'll talk to another woman."

"My blessed redeemer, Morgan. You know I will. Come on, my son. Let's go and see what we have facing us now," Aunt Ruth said as she lifted herself from the chair and headed for the door.

Crossing the adjoining yard, Aunt Ruth and Morgan both walked in silence, trying to process what they were about to encounter. It was almost too much to take in, without seeing for oneself, and Morgan could only speculate on what he was about to show his aunt after what had taken place the night before. As he pulled the latch on the door and entered the porch, he saw that both the girl and the blanket that had covered her were gone from the floor. She was now sitting in his mother's rocking chair by the window with the quilt wrapped snugly around her shoulders. The braid from the night before hung smooth and glossy down her neck as she was staring out the window, focused on the land across the bay. The land toward Dead Man's Cove.

Aunt Ruth looked up at Morgan questioningly and then, jutting out her chin as she straightened her shoulders in feistiness, she crossed the kitchen floor toward the young girl. Pulling out a chair from the table, she sat her rotund body beside the rocking chair and placed her hand on the shoulder of the unfamiliar person in front of her. Taking her eyes off the scene outside the window, the young woman turned towards Aunt Ruth and smiled.

"Hello, my dear. My name is Ruth," Morgan's aunt

said loudly, pointing her finger towards her ample bosom as if to make her words more understandable to the stranger.

Unexpectedly, the girl's smile brightened and pointing her finger toward herself she answered in a soft voice, "Alasie. Me Alasie."

CHAPTER FIVE

Although it was soon discovered that Alasie was limited in her vocabulary, she was still able to communicate enough to make herself understood. This alone gave Morgan reason to believe that she had indeed been in contact with the English before. But there was still so much about this mysterious woman he still did not know.

"You know how to speak some words in my language. Where did you learn it from?" Morgan inquired

"Alasie with white man. Learn talk."

"So you lived with an English family?"

"Not family. Bad man!"

"Oh!"

"Alasie not want talk about bad man." She lowered her head away from Morgan's gasping stare.

"Listen. You don't have to worry about anything bad happening here. You will be fine in Mam's old bedroom."

"Alasie know Morgan good. Alasie work at house. Cook. Clean."

"You do what you want here at home, but I have to

go fishing." Morgan pointed out towards the sea. Alasie nodded her understanding.

To Morgan it was such a change from the normal and it still baffled him as to how he should deal with it. But he knew one thing with sincere certainty, that it was his place to see that Alasie was cared for. He also knew that his Aunt Ruth didn't see it in the same way as he did as his frustrated, yet determined mind, wandered back to the first time he had argued with his aunt, concerning Alasie.

***

"Morgan, you know something has to change with your living arrangements," Aunt Ruth spoke with determination in her voice. She had come down to the stage, where Morgan was busy baiting his gear for the next day's fishing.

"We are fine, Aunt Ruth. I am not going to tell Alasie that she has to go somewhere else. I can't do that," Morgan declared, also with a hint of the same determination as his aunt. He didn't want to argue about what he felt was his own private business, but this was one time when Morgan knew he had to stand his ground with his aunt.

"Well, you are going to have to! You two can't be living alone together in your mother's house. What will the people in the harbour say? Your dear old mother would roll over in her grave if she knew that you were living in her house in sin, for God's sake!" Aunt Ruth fairly shouted at Morgan as if he were a disobedient child.

Her nonsensical tirade was as much as Morgan could take, as he lost control of his temper. "Living in sin? What do you think I am doing, Aunt Ruth? And as for what this harbour thinks, it is absolutely none of their God damn business." He knew he should not be losing control like this, but at this very moment he felt that what he was doing was the right thing. "And as for it being Mam's house, Mam is dead and gone. And what you don't know is that Mam knew that all this was going to happen. She told me the night she died," Morgan raged on.

Aunt Ruth's face looked like it was about to explode. Her jaw hung open and her hands were plastered to her generous bosom as she gasped at Morgan's outrageous statement.

"What in God's name are you getting on with my son? Your poor mother couldn't utter a word before she died. I'm sure she never told you about an Indian woman coming here and living in her house." Aunt Ruth was flustered and could not believe what foolishness Morgan was spewing.

"Never mind what I said," Morgan recanted, knowing how idiotic it must have sounded. "But you can tell anyone who thinks that what is happening in *my* house is sinful, that they can mind their own business because my business is my own and I don't need anybody telling me what I should or shouldn't be doing. That is the end of it," Morgan stormed, as he pointed to the stage door. "Go home, Aunt Ruth!"

Swinging her ample hips around, his aunt blew through the open stage door like an abrupt gust of wind as she stomped her way back toward her house.

Morgan had the makings of a headache for the rest of the day. He normally didn't lose his temper, but he knew that this time it had been called for. He just hoped that

Aunt Ruth would leave well enough alone. But he also knew with her penchant for gossip, the exaggerated details of this heated debate would soon be flying around Cape La Hune faster than snowflakes in a blizzard.

***

"I have to go back fishing tomorrow," Morgan told Alasie, as they sat across the supper table from one another. He pointed out the window towards the bay and pulled his arm back and forth, denoting a jigging motion.

Alasie nodded, understanding what Morgan meant. "Alasie, go medicine," she replied, pointing towards the hills above the community.

Morgan was not sure he understood what she was trying to tell him. "Medicine? There's no medicine up on those hills," he responded, as his questioning eyes stared at her, awaiting an explanation.

Alasie reached down to the floor with a picking motion. Then pointed at the floor. "Medicine," she answered his questioning stare.

Morgan realized that Alasie meant to gather plants that she would use as medicine and nodded. He had heard that this type of healing was done by Indians, but he knew very little, if anything about it. "I don't know how my Aunt Kitty, our old nursemaid, will feel about it, but you do what you need to," Morgan prattled on as Alasie just smiled and nodded.

After the dishes were cleared from the table, cleaned, and put away, Morgan sat back on the daybed in the cozy kitchen with a cup of tea. He had poured up one for Alasie as well, who was sitting in the old rocking chair that seemed to have become her favorite place. She placed the cup and saucer on the windowsill as she stared out at the now familiar sight of the bay.

"You still haven't told me where you came from," Morgan spoke with hesitance in his voice. "You mentioned a bad man, but you haven't said anything more about how you ended up here in Cape La Hune."

Both he and Aunt Ruth had asked the same question before, but up until now Alasie had given no response. Her usual reaction to the question was to turn and walk away without a word, always toward the beach on the northern side of the community.

"I'm not prying," Morgan softly whispered. "I am just trying to understand how you showed up here. Why here? Why to my house?" Morgan's throat started to fill up with raw emotion, as he asked the questions he really wanted to know the answers to. "Did you know my mother? Did you and she have a secret that I don't know about?"

The kitchen felt like a chamber that was closing in around Morgan. He felt a cold sweat trickling down his back, and his heartbeat was resonating in his head. Alasie stopped rocking and turned her tearstained face toward Morgan. She rose from the chair and crossed the old wood floor without a sound, as if she were a feather floating on the wind. Tears continued to flow like tiny rivers down her broad face and dropped from her strong ridged jawbone like raindrops. Her tiny hand reached out to stroke Morgan's face in a sensual gesture that seemed to hold compassion within its palm. She smiled sadly as she continued to caress the line of his jaw. Her ebony eyes stared lovingly at him as she whispered, "Not. Time."

Bending toward him, she brought her lips toward Morgan's and kissed him with a touch as light as the wind from a butterfly wing. Then, reaching for his hand, she led him up the narrow stairway and toward Morgan's bedroom.

CHAPTER SIX

Morgan had never felt as confused or as happy as he did that next day as he sat aboard his dory, with the calm ocean surrounding him, freshly caught cod in the bottom of his boat and a woman waiting for him at home. Yet, his mind was so mystified with the prospect of the very recent changes in his life, he was unsure what to really think of it all. The night before had been so inconceivable to Morgan that even a day ago, he could not imagine the impossibility. But his experiences thus far with Alasie had all been so unquestionably perfect, today he knew it was what he could no longer deny wanting in his life.

Morgan could still feel Alasie's body tangled with his own and her silken tresses caressing them both as they melded together in an exquisite knot of love and passion. Morgan's concept of love had been forever changed as his mind was overtaken by an emotion that,until now, had been completely alien to him. Alasie did that to him. She had sent Morgan's mind into a tailspin unlike anything he had ever known before.

An image of Alasie was transfixed in his mind's eye

from that morning when Morgan had arisen before dawn and eased himself out from under the warm quilts. Gazing at the unfamiliar scene of a woman in his bed, what he saw was a vision of perfection. Alasie lay so still with her black silken hair spread out in complete contrast to the snow-white pillow. The blue light from the moon shone its luminous radiance across the bedroom capturing the curve of Alasie's breast, as if it were jealous of Morgan who had caressed her satin flesh just hours before.

"God help me. I have never felt like this in my life," Morgan said aloud. "I don't know what to think about what is going on."

Grabbing the oars, he twisted the boat around and headed toward the harbour. He was looking forward to seeing Alasie and at the same time finding out for certain if what he thought to be real was actually some unfathomable dream.

CHAPTER SEVEN

After scrubbing out the boat, washing the fish and packing them in salt, the last chore was to moor the dory off from the wharf and secure everything on the stagehead. Morgan had baited the gear for the next day and was looking forward to seeing Alasie. His mind had been wandering all day to what had happened between them the night before. The union between Alasie and himself was something that Morgan had not anticipated, but now that it had occurred, he realized that he had subconsciously been wanting it all his life.

Walking up the well-trodden path toward his house, Morgan wondered what Alasie had spent her day doing. The day before she had filled the wood box from the pile of spruce and birch that was behind the house. She had also filled the water barrel.

He smiled as he remembered giving her his mother's clothes to wear a few days earlier. Alasie was about the same size as his mother and Morgan knew that she could not continue dressing in the tablecloth she had redesigned.

Pulling out the drawer from the small bureau in his mother's room, Morgan reached down and took out one of a few dresses that it contained. Passing it to Alasie, Morgan said, "This is for you," as he handed the simple blue dress to her.

Alasie took the dress and held it in front of herself. She looked back at Morgan with a smile and before he could say anything else, she whipped off the tablecloth, standing as naked as a newborn baby in front of him.

"Ahh, ohhh, blessed Jesus!" Morgan stammered as he turned to face the wall of the small room. He felt the heat rise to his face and was dumbstruck by the boldness of the spirited woman who was now occupying his home with him.

Feeling a light tap on his shoulder, Morgan turned around. Alasie stood there in what had been for his mother, a plain blue cotton dress. But the same dress on Alasie looked so much different. It was still plain, blue cotton, but it hugged her in all the right places.

A smile brightened her face as she twirled around in her bare feet on the painted plank flooring.

Morgan, embarrassed by what was going through his mind, pointed toward the drawer and in a flustered voice said, "Take what you need, they're yours now." He could not get out of the room fast enough.

Smiling at the recent memory, Morgan pulled the latch on the door and entered the kitchen. His first thought was that the house felt cold. Going to the stove and lifting the cover, he saw that there had been no fire lit and that the stove was cold to the touch. It looked as if no one had been at the house all day. Morgan had a sick feeling in his stomach like he had swallowed something heavy now lodged in his gut. Heading quickly up the stairs, he practically ran down the hallway to his bedroom, the place where he had last seen Alasie. The bed was empty and the quilt was neatly hauled up over the pillow where Alasie had laid the night before.

"Where in the name of God, is she gone?" Morgan spoke out loud to the empty room. "She must have gone over to Aunt Ruth's." He headed down the stairs and across the yard.

He hadn't spoken to Aunt Ruth since their disagreement about the living arrangements between Alasie and himself. He knew she might still be upset, but that wasn't the point right now. He just needed to know where Alasie had gone. So, pinning his hopes on Aunt Ruth not kicking him out, which he knew was highly unlikely, he pulled on the door latch and entered the warm, pleasant-smelling kitchen. Aunt Ruth and Naomi Jane were both sitting in the kitchen knitting. Morgan smelt the aroma of baking bread coming from the oven and there was a pot of something just as aromatic emanating from the stovetop.

Upon seeing him, Aunt Ruth dropped her knitting in her lap. "Well, look who decided to darken my door. I didn't know if you would come over here anymore after getting so mad at me yesterday."

"Don't be so foolish, Aunt Ruth. Everybody has arguments but that's not going to stop me from coming here," Morgan reasoned. "But that's not even why I'm here. Have either of you seen Alasie today? She isn't over to the house and the fire hasn't been going in the stove today either." Morgan's brow was furrowed with worry lines.

"Gilbert was just here having lunch and he spoke about seeing her going up the hill towards the graveyard early this morning," Naomi Jane stated. "I just heard him mention it when he was on his way out the door."

Neither Naomi Jane nor Aunt Ruth repeated Gilbert's actual statement that was essentially, 'Morgan's bloody old Indian was making her way up over the hills and as far as he was concerned it was good riddance to bad garbage.'

Morgan's face lit up with relief as remembered Alasie telling him last night at supper that she was going to get some medicine on the hills today.

"Suppose she's gone now that she got all your mother's clothes and her stuff. You might never see her again," Aunt Ruth firmly expressed her true feelings with a nod of her head.

"She's not gone!" Morgan articulated, in a voice that was a bit harsher than he intended. He didn't know what his aunt had against Alasie but whatever it was, she needed to get over it. "I just remembered that last night at supper she spoke about gathering medicine today. So, she's gone upon the hills to find what she needs."

"Up on the hills to get medicine?" Naomi Jane asked with sincere curiosity. Unlike her mother, she seemed intrigued and interested in Alasie. "What kind of medicine?"

Aunt Ruth, in her tendency to make herself heard at any cost, cut in before Morgan had a chance to reply. "What in the name of God do she think she is going to find up there! Medicine?! Foolishness is all that is. Indians, thinking they are doctors. Good God! If she thinks anyone here is going to let her put her hands on them with that witchcraft she must be off her head. I'm sure Kitty won't..."

"That's enough, Aunt Ruth! I won't listen to another word — and if you don't let up on Alasie, you might *not* see me over here again!" Morgan shouted as he slammed the wood door behind him. Leaving the two women in stunned silence.

Morgan's temper had again got the best of him, because of the unbelievable antics of his aunt. Grabbing a few pieces of kindling as he entered the porch, Morgan lifted the cover from the stovetop and shoved the wood in. Proceeding to strike a match to light it, Morgan snapped two of the wooden matches into pieces. Taking a couple of deep breaths, he tried to calm the fury that Aunt Ruth set off in him. Finally getting the match lit and the fire starting to whip around and flicker with the shaved wood, Morgan found his mind was still a jumble of harsh thoughts. For the life of him, he could not figure out the reason behind his aunt's dislike of this new person who had just entered their lives.

Morgan heaved a sigh of relief, at least he now knew where Alasie had gone... sort of. There were many places she could go once she reached the top of the hill, but Morgan trusted she would know her way. She seemed to be quite capable, and she did show up here out of nowhere, so she must have come from the mountains somewhere. There was no other way to get to Cape La Hune, other than across the bay, and she didn't have a boat so that was impossible. Or at least it was in Morgan's mind.

Busying himself in the kitchen, Morgan decided to fry up a fish that he had caught while out in the boat that day. He figured Alasie could certainly use a good meal when she got back home. "A pan of buns won't go to waste either," Morgan said to himself. The white alarm clock on the shelf showed three-thirty. Still about two more hours of daylight left, he thought to himself. Alasie should be walking through the door any time now.

CHAPTER EIGHT

He was sure he would soon have a path worn in the floor of the kitchen, but Morgan continued to pace the plank flooring. Darkness had cast its shadow across the tiny outport of Cape La Hune several hours ago and still there was no sign of Alasie. The fish and potatoes that Morgan had cooked earlier that evening had now dried up on the tail end of the stove as they had awaited to halt a hunger that he was sure would be rumbling in Alasie's stomach by this time. His hands had become red from having continuously rubbed them together as he walked the short distance from one end of the kitchen to the other.

His heart pounded in his throat as his mind raced through scenario after scenario of reasons that could be keeping Alasie away for this long. With each image growing worse than the next, Morgan finally raced outside to gulp down several breaths of the cool night air. He felt faint as he leaned over the bridge railing and vomited the contents of his stomach on the sandy gravel below. Wiping his mouth on the sleeve of his shirt, he looked toward the hills that he knew had been the trail Alasie had taken early that morning.

"Lord Jesus!? You just took Mam from me and now you are going to take the best thing that ever happened to me as well! What have I ever done to deserve this!?" Morgan raged at the starry sky above the tiny abode. After taking another few breaths to try and calm his rattled nerve, Morgan knelt on the roughly hewn planks of the bridge. He could feel the ripples and lines of the bare wood press into his kneecaps. Looking heavenward, with fingers crossed like the braided locks of Alasie's hair, Morgan's voice floated like a soft whisper on the wind. "Please, Lord. Please?"

The touch of a tear travelling down his cheek felt like Alasie's soft hand.

***

The squeaking of springs from the daybed startled Morgan awake just as dawn was breaking in the eastern sky. He had fallen asleep on the couch in the kitchen out of sheer exhaustion. Like the flicking of a switch, Morgan's mind instantly snapped to Alasie. Jumping up, he headed to the porch door to have a look outside.

There in the middle of the porch was a pair of his mother's old boots that Alasie had taken to wearing and a flour sack that bulged from whatever was inside. Racing up the stairs and down the hallway, Morgan's relief was finally alleviated by the sight of Alasie, sound asleep in the bed. Her hair was still in its familiar braid with wispy strands feathering her cheek. Hands that had just yesterday caressed his body, were clasped together and rested underneath her head.

With a sigh of utter relief, Morgan's body felt weak from the sudden drop of adrenaline. Backing slowly from the room, so as not to make any unintentional noise that would disturb her, he creeped across the hallway and slowly down the staircase. The sun was rising higher in the sky and filling the kitchen in a golden stream of brilliant luminosity. Morgan's heart felt that same glow.

***

The old, white clock on the shelf showed nine o'clock when Morgan heard a squeak from the floorboards upstairs. He had boiled two eggs and set them aside for Alasie earlier that morning, guessing that she would have to be virtually starving by this time. As he heard her ascending the stairs, he poured up a steaming cup of tea for them both from the porcelain pot on the stove, as he readied the meal that would finally break her fast.

"Good morning, sleepy head." He smiled as Alasie entered the kitchen holding the bulging flour sack. "You must be starving after being gone all yesterday?" He rubbed his stomach to make himself understood.

"Eat. Yesterday," she replied.

"What did you eat? I couldn't see anything missing that you would have taken with you."

"Food. On. Mountain," she replied, making a motion of picking up something from the floor and putting it in her mouth.

"So... what you are saying is that you picked things... berries, or whatever and ate them?" He nodded his head with understanding.

Alasie nodded as well.

"Well, berries or whatever may have been fine yesterday, but I've still got your breakfast ready for you this morning," he indicated her place by the table where the rocking chair awaited her.

Morgan had just sat across the table from Alasie and raised his teacup to his lips when a woman's panicked voice could be heard coming from outside. "Morgan? Oh, Morgan!"

Nearly dropping the cup as he jumped up from the table, Morgan rushed to the door with Alasie close behind him.

Naomi Jane was running across the yard when he pushed open the door. She was as white as a ghost, and tears were streaming down her face.

"What's wrong?" Morgan knew it was something he wasn't going to want to hear, seeing the fear in Naomi Jane's face.

"It's Peter. He chopped his leg with the axe!" Naomi Jane cried. "The axe went right in his leg."

Morgan only heard the first part of the explanation as he was tearing off across the yard toward the house next door with Alasie racing just inches behind him.

Peter was laying on the daybed of Aunt Ruth's kitchen, with his pant leg hiked up over his shin when Morgan and Alasie got there. A slow trickle of blood was flowing from the open wound and down onto the snow-white sheet that had been placed underneath his leg.

Aunt Ruth was sitting on a chair by the table wiping her flushed face with a cloth. "He's gonna die! Oh my blessed redeemer. Our poor little Peter!" Aunt Ruth wailed frantically.

Morgan dropped to his knees beside the daybed and placed his hand on Peter's shoulder. "Well, well Peter. What did you do this time?" Morgan smiled as he tried to comfort the young boy. He was sure Aunt Ruth with all her doom and gloom pretty much had the poor child frightened to death by this time.

"I chopped my leg with the axe that dad sharpened yesterday," Peter choked out. "He told me to be careful with it, but I guess I wasn't careful enough."

"Don't you worry, it doesn't seem to be bleeding too bad and I am sure Aunt Kitty will have you fixed up in no time," Morgan told him, referring to his aunt who served as the community nurse. For years, she was the only person with any sort of medical knowledge the community had to depend on.

"Aunt Kitty went to Cul de Sac the day before yesterday to birth a baby down there. The woman's husband came up and got her in the dory," Aunt Ruth bawled. "Aunt Kitty's not here and now poor little Peter is going to bleed to death!"

Not able to take any more of Aunt Ruth's hysterics, Morgan jumped up from the floor and grabbed hold of Aunt Ruth's arm, passing her off to Naomi Jane. "Can you take her out on the bridge? She isn't doing anyone any good here, especially Peter."

As Morgan turned back toward Peter to see what was to be done next to help the boy, he was surprised to see Alasie kneeling by the bed, rummaging through the flour sack bag that she had brought with her.

For the next while, Morgan and Naomi Jane, who had returned to be with her son, were amazed by how Alasie handled the circumstances that had befallen the child.

Rising from the floor, Alasie went to the counter and retrieved a bowl and filled it with water from the kettle on the stove. She ripped a piece from the cotton sheet that had been placed underneath the child's leg and soaked it in the warm water before she gently wiped the blood and dirt from the open cut.

Peter moaned quietly, as his mother wiped away the tear stains from his tiny face.

After Alasie had cleaned the wound, she pulled what looked like leaves from the flour sack. Placing them into her palm she rubbed them into a soft wad and packed them into the cut. Morgan could have sworn they were leaves from the crackberry plants that grew wild all over the area.

Once again reaching into her bag, Alasie pulled out a glass jar that she must have taken from the house before she went on her medicine hunt. Upon opening the jar, the familiar, woodsy scent of balsam fir sap wafted through the kitchen. Pointing to Morgan and then to the cut, she said, "Help. Push." Morgan knelt beside her and gently pushed the wound together as Alasie spread a mixture over the cut.

Peter cried out as the cut was pushed together and Naomi Jane looked hard at Morgan. "You're hurting him!"

Alasie gently put her hand over Naomi Jane's hand as she whispered with a soft smile, "Not. Hurt. Help."

Naomi Jane saw a true sense of caring in the eyes of the otherwoman and knew that she could trust her son's caregiver to do what was needed to help her boy.

Alasie rose from the floor and headed out the door of the porch without a word.

"Where has she gone?" Naomi Jane asked Morgan with a bewildered look.

"Your guess is as good as mine," Morgan replied, not even able to guess what Alasie was doing or what would be next in her arsenal of medicinal knowledge.

"Where did she learn to do all this and what were those leaves she was using?" Naomi Jane inquired as to what she had just witnessed.

Morgan just shrugged his shoulders. "I'm just as amazed as you are and I don't have any idea where she learned to do this."

Just then Alasie came back into the kitchen with a large piece of paper-thin birch bark. Lifting Peter's leg just a fraction, she pulled out the sheet that had been placed underneath it. She placed the sheet of birch bark on top of the cut like a covering, then ripping the end off the sheet, she proceeded to wrap the boy's leg in the cotton bandage.

Standing by the daybed, after the bandaging was done, Alasie turned to Naomi Jane.

"Not. Move." Holding up her five fingers in reference to a time period, she also added, "Suns."

"If I understand right, you mean you want Peter to stay there for five days?" Naomi Jane asked.

Alasie nodded and pointed to herself. "Check. Boy. Five. Suns."

As Alasie took her bag and turned to leave, Naomi Jane wrapped her arms around Alasie, hugging her in a tight embrace. "I don't know what we would have done without you today. You are a Godsend, and I am so grateful that you were here and for what you just did for Peter."

Alasie smiled at the worried mother and taking her bag, she headed back across the yard to the home she now shared with Morgan.

CHAPTER NINE

After what had been a very tiring day, Morgan and Alasie were both relaxing by the kitchen table. He blew on the tea in his cup to cool it down before tasting it. Alasie had taken the contents of her medicinal flora out of the flour sack and had them spread out across the white tablecloth as she precisely arranged them in small bundles. Morgan was watching intently and recognized some of the plants as ones he had seen before but had never recognized them as being used as a type of medicine.

He'd known it before, but he was once again recognizing that this unique individual, sitting across from him, would change his life in ways he could never imagine.

A sudden bang of the porch door startled both Morgan and Alasie from the quiet of the room. Gilbert's frame filled the doorway of the kitchen like a beast on a rampage. His reddened face was bulging to the point of exploding and the air around him reeked of gut-rot alcohol and sour sweat. His coal black hair was matted to his head with the rivulets of perspiration that was running down his large forehead.

"What the hell did you do to my boy today?" Gilbert swore in rage as he pointed his large finger directly at Alasie.

"What are you getting on about, Gilbert? Alasie did what needed to be done for the chop in Peter's leg," Morgan replied as he got up from where he was sitting to face the enraged man.

"Needed to be done!? How the hell do you think that God-damn Indian knows anything about fixing my boy's leg? Plugging leaves and bark and god knows what in it. He'll probably lose his leg and perhaps kill him!" Gilbert roared.

"Now just a minute, Gilbert," Morgan intercepted. He realized he was dealing with a drunken man who did not appreciate the help that had generously been offered earlier that day, so trying to calm his voice, he continued: "I'm not having you come into my house swearing and screaming at Alasie. All she did was try and help your boy. She didn't cause any harm to anybody. Now I think you should leave."

"Oh, I'll leave, but you remember to keep that Indian bed warmer on your side of the yard. The way I got it figured out, she knows as much about doctoring as I do about the moon," Gilbert's speech was slurred from his intoxication, and spittle ran down over his chin.

"Have it your own way, Gilbert. But you may live to regret those words one day," Morgan replied, as he closed the door behind the drunken man.

Crossing the kitchen and taking Alasie in his arms, he held her close to his racing heart. Expecting her to be upset, Morgan was surprised when she pulled away from him. Looking directly into his eyes and with a voice of sheer determination she said, "Alasie. Must. Teach. Medicine."

CHAPTER TEN

"Anybody here?" Aunt Kitty hollered as she waddled her big frame through Morgan's kitchen door.

"Alasie. Here," she replied, whirling around from the counter where she was cleaning the soot from the flues of the kerosene lamps.

"You are just the one who I am looking for. I'm Kitty — well, I guess if you're going to be living here with Morgan, you might as well call me Aunt Kitty too," she announced as an introduction of herself. "It's time to see about Peter's leg. Take your stuff and we'll go over to the house and see how everything is with young Peter," Aunt Kitty announced to an astonished Alasie.

"Alasie not go. Man mad with Alasie. I no see boy."

"Yes, my maid, I know all about what that thick headed dunce did, coming over here loaded drunk and cursing on you. What you don't know is that that same bloody fool is my son and he is just like his poor old father."

Alasie stared at Aunt Kitty with a shocked expression on her face.

"I see you are able to understand what I say but you

can't talk so well," Aunt Kitty smiled. "Yes, my dear. That's my boy that went off on you like the devil himself. He ain't got a grain of common sense in that noggin at all, and on top of that, he loves his drink. The blood of the devil I call it. He's the spitting image of his father." Aunt Kitty plopped her overly large frame on the chair next to the kitchen door. Using the end of her flour sack apron, she wiped the perspiration that was beading on her forehead. "People wonder why I am blunt about things and why I won't take any foolishness from anybody. Well, I can tell you: when you have lived with men like Gilbert and his father Amos, you had enough foolery to deal with under your own roof, let alone having to put up with it when you are trying to do some good under someone else's. Some of the stuff I have seen done over the years would almost make you think that a chicken had more brains than some people."

Alasie handed Aunt Kitty a glass of water from the jug on the counter. The old woman looked flushed and seemed a bit out of breath. "There you go, my dear. You know what I needed by just looking at me," Aunt Kitty laughed. "Don't you give no heed to the crowd around here. Some of them don't know their head from their ass yet. But you do," Aunt Kitty winked. "Naomi Jane told me what you did with Peter's leg. I can't say I've ever done it that way, but I know you have, and I bet you a dime to a dollar that leg is healing just like it should be." Placing her hands on the table, Aunt Kitty struggled to raise her body from the chair. "As you can see, I am not getting any younger and if those people living here want to be looked out for, then they better damn well learn who knows best. And that, my dear, might just be you."

Alasie blushed at the unexpected compliment she was receiving from the most unusual person she had ever met; yet she felt that "Aunt" Kitty would be a friend she desperately needed.

Reaching behind the kitchen door, Alasie unhooked the white pillowcase that had been hanging on a nail. She slung the bag that was now known as the medicine bag over her shoulder and followed Aunt Kitty out into the yard.

"By the way. You won't have to worry about Aunt Ruth blabbering all this to Gilbert when he comes in from fishing. That woman has a tongue that flaps worse than a flag in a gale of north-east wind," Aunt Kitty laughed at her own joke. "I have already told her that if she says anything at all about you helping Peter again, I will make sure that the minister has a little talk with her about gossiping when he comes around next time. I can tell you now, that will put a lot less flap in that tongue of hers."

***

"Well, I must say, what you've done for my grandson's leg seems to be working like a charm," Aunt Kitty smiled at Alasie. "I would never have used bunchberry leaves to stop blood or the balsam sap to glue it together but by the look of this, you have used this remedy before, and you know how and where to get what you need. That's what I call using your head in the right way."

Naomi Jane hugged Alasie. "You can take that as a big compliment because Aunt Kitty doesn't give those to many people," she whispered into Alasie's ear.

Alasie smiled and returned the hug.

"Now, so as not to tempt fate with Gilbert and his bloody foolishness again, I want you to show me exactly what I need to do so that I can continue the care and you not get your head bitten off again," Aunt Kitty proposed.

"I am so sorry about what Gilbert did. Coming over to your house all upset like that over nothing. I hope you know that I don't feel anything but friendship and thanks toward you, Alasie. I am just so very, very grateful you were here and knew what to do for my boy," Naomi Jane spoke to Alasie with her head hung down in shame.

Alasie reached out and lifted Naomi Jane's face to look into her eyes.

"Not worry. He not got lot there," Alasie laughed, and pointed to her head. "Aunt Kitty say like chicken."

Naomi Jane giggled and nodded her head in total agreement.

"That's right, my girl, no more brains than a chicken." Aunt Kitty chuckled. "Gilbert could use a good dose of common sense, and not the kind of sense that comes from a liquor bottle."

"Thank you so much, Alasie, for what you have done. I haven't got anything much to give you for helping but I did bake some pork buns for you." Naomi Jane handed Alasie a plate of fresh buns that had been just taken from the oven. The smell was mouthwatering and Alasie gratefully accepted the gift of thanks.

"You can bring a couple of those buns with you when you come down to my house after dinner," Aunt Kitty said, patting Alasie on the shoulder. "I will put the kettle on, and you and I are going to have a yarn. Oh, and don't forget that medicine bag of yours. This old dog might still be able to learn a trick or two yet."

CHAPTER ELEVEN

Over the next several weeks, Aunt Kitty and Alasie had many cups of tea and pork buns together. Aunt Kitty also found out that she still had the ability to be taught more than a few new tricks. It seemed to her that Alasie's medicine bag was like a magician's hat, and that each pull brought a brand new trick for her to learn. While each new day brought their relationship closer as well.

"Good day, Aunt Kitty," Florence Barter, the store's owner, greeted her cheerfully from behind the counter. Barter & Sons Ltd. was the one and only general store in Cape La Hune and, as Aunt Kitty was well aware of, it was also a place where you could get the latest town gossip along with your butter, sugar, and milk. "It's a beautiful day."

"Yes it is, but it's hot enough to roast you. How come you haven't got the door opened?" Aunt Kitty inquired.

"Well, to tell the God's Almighty truth, Aunt Kitty, I'm trying not to listen to all the sacrilegious talk that several of the men out on the step are going on about," Florence answered. She had forgotten that she had left the window slightly ajar where Aunt Kitty had seen her with her ear to the opening as she came down the road toward the store.

"I heard them when I was coming down the road. It's scandalous. Let the minister come and you'll see all of the harbour's gossipmongers in their pews, acting as if butter wouldn't melt in their mouth. Then ten minutes after the church door is shut, they're all back in their little gathering spots spreading lies and tattling tales again."

"That poor woman that Morgan has up there must have the ears burned right off the sides of her head by this time," Florence said, shaking her head in mock disgust as she tried to edge Aunt Kitty into giving her any little tidbit she could pass on down the line to whoever would listen. "The stuff that they have said about her is enough to make the devil blush." Florence leaned over the counter toward Aunt Kitty and lowered her voice. "I don't know if I would want her tending to me if I was sick, but for those men out there," she continued, pointing to several of the community's male occupants that were gathered outside the storefront, "what they are saying is utterly shameful. That's why I am suffering here in this heat, rather than listen to all that smut." Florence exaggerated her statement as she took a paper fan from underneath the counter and flapped it in the air to cool her pinched face.

"I can tell you one thing, Florence. If I get sick, you can believe me when I say that "that girl" better be the one tending to me. Now you are hearing this right from the horse's mouth," Aunt Kitty announced unashamedly. "She, and by the way her name is Alasie, has more common sense in her little finger then the whole crowd of you gossipers all put together," she said, pointing out the window at the male gathering and then bringing her arthritic finger around to point directly at Florence. "Now here is eleven cents," Aunt Kitty slapped the coins on the wooden counter. "Do your job and get me a pound of tea, instead of trying to get any news you can spread around the harbour out of me today," she voiced loudly with all the purposeful intention she could muster.

Florence Barter, flustered and embarrassed, quickly scooped out Aunt Kitty's tea from the open box and wrapped it as quickly as she could, trying to get rid of her feisty customer.

Leaving the store with the brown paper sack tied in white cotton string, Aunt Kitty opened the door and turned back toward Florence. With a voice loud enough to be heard by all the men gathered outside, she gave what would be Florence's hard lesson in gossiping. "As for that itching and burning you had down there," Aunt Kitty pointed toward her feminine area, "mash up eight or ten partridge berries in a glass of warm water two or three times a day and drink that. Make sure you scrub really well and that will get rid of that smell too." Aunt Kitty wrinkled up her nose. "You'll be cured before you know it. And if you want to know how I know that, "Alasie" told me."

Then turning as fast as her hefty frame would allow, Aunt Kitty slammed the door and left the store with a red-faced and mortified Florence staring at her from behind the counter.

As the door slammed, the men that had been listening to Aunt Kitty's commentary from outside the store turned toward her, not really knowing what to say.

"It's a nice day, Aunt Kitty," one of the grizzled looking fishermen finally greeted her.

"Yes, and it would be a better one if some people did something worthwhile instead of sitting on their lazy asses talking about stuff they don't know the first thing about," Aunt Kitty loudly announced, as she pointed her rheumatic finger at the crowd of stunned men.

"What the hell is up the leg of your drawers today?" one of the men asked, rolling his eyes at the others.

"I'll have you know, my drawers have nothing to do with you, just like what you're all gossiping about don't have nothing to do with you either." Aunt Kitty stood on the shop step staring at each of the men and tempting them to say something against her. "I would say the minister needs to preach a sermon about 'do unto others'," she continued. "Perhaps one of you can offer your services to the church and lay-read next Sunday?"

Stepping down and breaking up the gathering with a push, Aunt Kitty proceeded toward her house with an old, familiar spring in her step and a smile on her face.

CHAPTER TWELVE

Chomp! Bang!

The large, rusty knife hit the slub, splattered bench where Morgan was cutting up bait for tomorrow's fishing trawl. As he slid the last pieces of herring into the bucket, Morgan sighed with relief. It had been a long day and though his catch was good, he was tired from the day's work in the warm sun. Grabbing another pail, he headed to the edge of the wharf to draw a bucket of salt water to wash down the wooden bench. As he neared the door, he could hear several women on a nearby flake chatting as they turned salt fish to keep it from burning in the summer sun. Morgan's ears perked up when he heard the words "Morgan's Indian woman". Retracing his steps to stand hidden behind the stage door, he couldn't help but listen to what was being spoken about Alasie.

"Well, I, for one, think it is a wonderful thing. Aunt Kitty says she knows what she is doing, and if that's the case, then I trust she knows enough if anything goes wrong with either one of my crowd," one woman spoke confidently.

"Yes, I see where you are coming from. But... I'm still not sure I want an Indian trying to make me better if I was sick," replied another voice.

"Indian or not, if she can fix up anybody belonging to me as well as Aunt Kitty said she fixed up Naomi Jane's young boy, then she's welcome in my house any time," a third voice said. "Did you see him; running around after only a month with not even so much as a limp. Sure, Aunt Kitty said herself at the church meeting the other night that she couldn't have done it as good."

"I don't think Aunt Kitty called that meeting as much for church business as she did for a medical meeting. You should have been there, Ethel. She even told us that there is a flower in most everybody's garden that can keep us from having so many babies. What was it that she called it, Irene?"

"Queen Ann's Lace," the woman laughed. "Can you imagine I've already had ten babies pushed through me, with the last three Jesus near killing me. And if that woman had been here years ago maybe my poor old twat wouldn't be stretched out like a wet worsted mitt."

There was a roar of laughter from the woman's off-colour remark.

"Can you imagine now, every time Jim puts it in me, I can take some flower seeds from the garden and push it out again," another voice laughed uncontrollably. "I don't know if it works like that girl says but I can tell you, I am damn well going to know. I already pushed out six and one of them was a set of twins."

One of the women, whose voice sounded younger and more timid, spoke up. "The bible says we should be thankful for what God gives us."

"I got nothing against the blessed Lord or what he says, but he hasn't got to carry a dozen babies or raise them. You got what... two so far? When you have your tenth one, come and talk to me about being grateful," said the voice, as the women walked away from the flake and toward their respective houses.

Morgan drew the bucket of water and finished cleaning the stage. Upon final inspection he grabbed his cram box and headed toward his house with an old, familiar spring in his step and a smile on his face.

***

Passing along by Aunt Kitty's limed, white bungalow, Morgan saw her sitting out on her bridge knitting. She held up her hand in a gesturing wave. Making his way up the gravel pathway, Morgan put down his cram box and seated himself on the step.

"How was the fish today?" Aunt Kitty inquired.

"Not too bad for this time of the year," answered Morgan with a cheerful note in his voice.

"That's good, my son. Do save me a meal of cod's heads the next time you get out."

"I'll do that tomorrow, Aunt Kitty," Morgan answered. As if deciding how to say what he had on his mind, Morgan gazed away and hesitated for a bit.

"You look like you want to say something, Morgan."

Swallowing to try and wet the inside of his suddenly dry throat. Morgan looked up at his Aunt Kitty. "What I want to say is thank you. Thank you for all you have done for Alasie. You've taken her under your wing, and she seems so happy," Morgan said softly.

"Look here, my son. That girl is smart, very smart, but she is also different and that makes it hard for people to accept her. I don't want to condemn my own people, but it is hard for people to change and that's what accepting Alasie into this community means," Aunt Kitty gently but firmly replied.

"I know it is a lot for people to take in, but she is so good and I've never been happier in my life."

"You don't have to tell me that, Morgan, because I can see it when I look at you. I've taken to the girl too but there is something different about her. I can't put my finger on it but there is more to her then we know," Aunt Kitty responded, as she thoughtfully shook her head.

Morgan hesitated for the second time, wondering if what he was about to tell Aunt Kitty would be believed by the woman. He knew Aunt Kitty was not going to heed any nonsense from anyone, even himself, but in Morgan's mind this was what he trusted as the honest to God's truth.

"Can I tell you something very private, Aunt Kitty? Something I don't want you to ever tell anybody else." Aunt Kitty nodded her head as she stared sincerely at Morgan. "Maybe you will think I am gone off my head, but I think Mam knew Alasie before we all did. At least she knew she was coming here."

"How do you think your mother, my dear sister, knew about an Indian girl?" Aunt Kitty stared at Morgan in all seriousness, knowing he would never utter such a profound statement without some significant explanation to back it up.

"Well, that's the thing. I don't know how she knew, but the night Mam passed away, I was sitting by her bed and she woke up for just a minute. She looked straight at me and she said the words, "She is coming" and that "I must love her;" then she lay back on the pillow and she was gone." Before Aunt Kitty could say anything, Morgan started to speak faster and with more earnestness in his voice. "I knows how this must sound and perhaps you think I am crazy, but I know what I seen and I know what I heard Mam say and...."

"Morgan!" Putting up her hand to stop his jabbering. "Slow down, my son. I just want to say that I believe you," Aunt Kitty gently whispered with a quiver in her voice.

"So you don't think I am crazy," Morgan responded with a heavy sigh of relief.

"I know you are not crazy. And, although I don't know exactly what happened in that room the night your poor mother passed on, what I do know is this. Over my many years tending to the sick and the dying, there have been many things that I have seen and many more that I have heard about from other people when somebody dies that can't be explained." Aunt Kitty shrugged her shoulders as she continued, "What I think is that we are not asked to explain them, but just to accept them for whatever reason they were given. So, whatever you think your mother knew or was trying to tell you, that is now up to you to accept or forget. That, Morgan, is your choice."

Morgan sat quietly on the step, contemplating the information, as well as the advice, given to him by his aunt. After a moment he rose, taking his cram box in his hand and turning to his aunt with a smile on his face.

"I know what I choose, Aunt Kitty. And I am going home to see her now."

CHAPTER THIRTEEN

Curled, dry leaves of scarlet and gold blew around the yard like dancers twirling on a ballroom floor, while angry waves capped in white paraded straight out the bay like soldiers marching off to war.

Fishing would be out of the question for today, but Morgan knew there were many other chores that he could think of that would fill his time.

"Morgan and Alasie dig in garden," Alasie announced. Looking up from his breakfast, Morgan laughed as Alasie entered the kitchen wearing a pair of rubbers and holding a hoe in her hand.

"I knew I would soon find something else to do today." Morgan couldn't help but grin at the would-be farmer standing before him.

"Alasie know how dig garden. Aunt Kitty show Alasie," she announced, proud of the new accomplishment. "Alasie show Aunt Kitty medicine, Aunt Kitty show Alasie much things," she explained to Morgan as she spread out her arms to portray the many undertakings she had learned from her mentor.

Alasie's English was improving day by day and now after four months, she had very little problem making herself understood.

"Get up, lazyass," Alasie snickered at Morgan. "We get at it," laughing as she headed out the door.

"Aunt Kitty has been teaching you too well, I think." Morgan smiled and shook his head as he followed 'his boss' toward the garden.

***

"Five, six, seven, eight, nine, ten. There are ten crates of potatoes, three crates of turnip, and three crates of carrots," Morgan announced to Alasie. "That will go quite a way towards the winter vegetables for us."

Alasie smiled as she looked at the harvest that came from the rich, black soil. She loved harvesting plants for medicine but harvesting food that they had grown themselves was a whole new experience, and one she was enjoying immensely.

"I have a couple of buckets of sand that are ready in the shed to store the carrots in for the winter," Morgan told Alasie. "Do you want to pick some of the cabbage greens for supper while I'm getting them?"

As she was about to answer Morgan's question, she swatted at a fly that was buzzing in her face. Forgetting that her hands were less than clean, Alasie swept a clot of the mud directly into her mouth.

"Yuck, blah!" Alasie hacked and coughed as she spat the black earth back to the ground where it belonged.

Morgan started laughing, "You look like a real farmer now. Mud covered from head to toe."

Alasie poked out her tongue at the would-be jokester, while Morgan laughed harder when he saw that Alasie's tongue was still black from the mud.

"Alasie go wash mud off hands, face," she said as she headed for the house.

"Don't forget your tongue too!" Morgan hollered, laughing as he headed to the shed.

Morgan had just returned from getting the sand for the carrots when he saw a lanky, young boy he knew running up the road waving his arms toward him. Dropping the heavy buckets to the ground, Morgan shouted, "What's the matter?"

"It's Dad!" the boy breathlessly panted. Morgan noticed a trickle of blood oozing from the corner of his lip. "Aunt Kitty wants the Indian to come down to the house with her," wheezed out the young lad.

Morgan felt a heated rage building up inside him from the disrespect this young lad was aiming toward Alasie, but he knew he had to let go of his anger for now. Alasie, having heard what the boy said, grabbed the white medicine bag from the nail behind the kitchen door and was soon hurrying down the road with it slung over her shoulder.

As he followed behind her, Morgan entered the home shortly after Alasie. The owner of the home, Pat Simms, a large, burly man, lay on the dirty plank floor, with his sizeable body spread out and covering most of the area of the small kitchen. Morgan guessed from the purple stain around his mouth and nose, Pat Simms was probably already dead. Alasie was kneeling beside him, with her ear to his chest while Aunt Kitty stood beside Gladys, his wife, with her arms wrapped around the woman's frail shoulders. Morgan saw that Gladys's eye was bruised and swollen shut. The chairs were overturned, and one had sharp wood spikes sticking up from a broken leg. Morgan could very easily imagine the recent happenings within the Simms' household. As he looked around the filthy little kitchen, the noxious odour of stale alcohol and urine fused in the thick, hot air of the small room to leave a lingering twinge in Morgan's nostrils. Several of the Simms children were in the room, witnessing the horrific scene playing out in front of them. One very young boy clung to his mother's apron wearing only a sagging diaper that from the smell alone indicated it needed changing. Another young girl with greasy brown hair and a dress that looked three times her size, was huddled in a rocking chair in the far corner, holding an infant who was screaming loudly. He knew that what these innocent children had seen happen in their full view that day would forever be attached to their tender minds and hitch a ride on their character for better or for worse.

Alasie arose from where she had been resting her ear on Pat's Simms's chest. Looking despondently at Aunt Kitty, she shook her head. Gladys' face turned a pasty grey as she started to slide towards the floor. Alasie righted an overturned chair, as Aunt Kitty lowered the now widowed woman to the seat. Reaching for a glass on the table and smelling its contents, Alasie passed what she hoped to be water to Gladys, patting the woman's hand.

"Not worry. Man gone to Great Spirit. He not hurt you any more," Alasie spoke gently as she reached up to lightly touch the woman's discoloured eye.

Gladys's head instantly sprang up as she slapped Alasie's hand away from her face. Looking directly into her eyes with utter disgust, she seethed with a voice full of venom, "Not hurt me!? What do you think you know about hurt? I have six mouths to feed and no husband," Gladys hissed as she pointed her finger in Alasie's face. "Do you think this hurts me?" She pointed to her bruised eye. "Well, this is nothing compared to having my family broken up. I'd put up with all the black marks that man was able to belt out, as long as my family was together." Gladys' anger was palpable as she cleared her throat and spat directly in Alasie's face.

Alasie stood rigidly, staring awestruck at the enraged woman as the spittle from Gladys' lips ran slowly down over her cheek.

"You, a bloody Indian, come into my house telling me about my husband hurting me and about spirits. Get the hell out of my house!" roared Gladys as she slowly slid off the chair and lay with her head on her dead husband's chest.

Wiping the spit from her face into the sleeve of her dress and grabbing up her medicine bag, Alasie tore past Morgan and toward the door. Once outside and tightly holding on to the rickety railing of the bridge, she gulped in breaths of the cool air. Morgan, who had exited the caustic dwelling directly behind Alasie, took her tenderly into his arms and held her close to his chest as the tears flowed down her face. A mournful wailing filled the air from inside the home.

CHAPTER FOURTEEN

Two hours after arriving back to the safety of their own home, Alasie still hadn't spoken a word. Morgan had tried several times to start a conversation, but she just sat silently in the rocking chair, staring out the window at the now familiar scene across the bay. The windy breeze from earlier that morning had now turned into a savage beast. It violently snatched the white caps from the waves as it blew them high into the air in smoky whirlwinds. Running to hell for leather, the monster slammed fiercely into whatever was in its path of destruction.

Morgan's mind was in full parallelism. The whirling of his thoughts was in total uniformity with the vortex of the storm and it was difficult to predict which would cause the most destruction.

He finally gave up the silence of the house and went down to the wharf to ensure that everything was okay in the storm.

John Rose, a fisherman who Morgan knew well, was also checking on things and upon finishing, walked over to the stage where Morgan had holed himself up.

"Lord Almighty! Is this ever going to let up?" John said rhetorically, as he grabbed the stage door that nearly blew out of his hand as he entered.

Morgan shook his head. "Seems like it's getting worse instead of getting better."

"Allen Simm' boat is swamped over on his mooring."

Morgan looked out of the dirty salt encrusted window toward the man's wharf. A buff-coloured dory full of water was just noticeable as the waves bellowed over the green gunnels.

"He was going to try and pull it ashore when his old lady came down screaming that his brother Pat was dead."

This was the very topic Morgan did not want to talk about, but it seemed to be forced upon him.

"Too bad, old man. Pat was a good fellow and with a big family."

Morgan didn't comment. He knew he could not answer honestly so it was better to keep his mouth shut.

"The wife was saying just now, how she pitied poor Gladys so much," John continued. "She was always so quiet-spoken and mild. She said you hardly ever saw her outside the house. It's a damn sin. A wonderful family broke up and a great man went way too early."

Morgan could not listen to another word. Trying to calm his thoughts by coming to his stage had now proven to have had the opposite effect, and Morgan's temper exploded.

"Great man!? John my son, you must have shit in your eyes."

John Rose stared at Morgan in surprise. But Morgan

wasn't close to finishing, and although he knew his friend wasn't to blame for his rage, John had definitely found himself in the wrong place at the wrong time as all hell broke loose inside of Morgan.

"Pat Simms was an alcoholic wife beater. He beat his wife, and he beat his children. The reason you didn't see Gladys was she didn't want anyone else seeing her black eyes and bruises. They lived in filth and as for meek and mild, you didn't see her spitfire attack on Alasie earlier today."

"Calm down, Morgan! These are pretty strong words you are saying about a dead man and his grieving family."

"Well, I'm only telling the truth. Don't expect me to praise Pat Simms now because he's dead. He wasn't a good man, and he did beat his family and that's the way it was. Yes, he's dead! And yes, Gladys might be grieving, but she is only grieving because she doesn't know what will happen to her and her children. If you think she's mourning Pat because she loved him, then you are just as big of a God-damn fool as the rest of this bloody community who will praise Pat Simms and call him good now he's dead."

"Morgan old boy, you need to calm down. I wouldn't let any of his family hear you say what you just told me. You might be asking for a good ass kicking if either of Pat's brothers gets a hold of that."

"Let them come and try," Morgan said. "I will tell them exactly like I told you. Ass kicking or not, the truth is the truth and when it involves treating Alasie like she was treated today, then it will be worth whatever they want to give me."

"Morgan, if this is all about your Indian woman, then…"

"Alasie! Her name is Alasie. And she is a good person, and she only tries to help people! Can't anyone in this harbour get that inside their thick skulls?!" Morgan was raging and his temper was beyond control as he violently ploughed his fist down on the splitting table. With a resounding crack, the board split into two pieces.

"I think it's time for me to go." John said, turning his back to leave. As he reached for the latch on the stage door, John dropped the final stone in the well. "I think you need to decide if 'that Indian' is worth losing your friends and family over."

As the door closed behind John Rose, the large chopping knife that was on the bait table simultaneously flew through the air like a shooting star. As its rusted blade stuck deep into the weathered wood of the door, Morgan's primitive roar could be heard over the savage storm that raged outside the tiny shed.

CHAPTER FIFTEEN

Morgan was disgusted at his loss of self control. He had let his temper go to the point of not recognizing himself and of what he was capable of doing. As he headed toward the limed, white house down the road, he knew this was the only place he could honestly talk to someone and get the advice he needed.

"Anyone home?" Morgan asked as he entered the warm inviting kitchen.

"I've been expecting I'd soon see you," Aunt Kitty said as she rose from her chair and came to put her large sagging arms around Morgan. "I know it has not been an easy day on any of us, but I think it has been especially hard on you."

"Harder than you even want to know, Aunt Kitty."

"I figured as much. Sit yourself down and let me pour us both a drink of brandy and warm water to calm our nerves."

"I definitely could use something to calm my nerves, but I didn't expect you to offer me alcohol."

"It's medicinal, Morgan, my boy. There is a world of

difference in drinking for the sake of getting drunk and drinking for relaxation. The first is evil and the second is balm for the soul."

Morgan lifted the glass that Aunt Kitty had placed in front of him. The steam that rose from the heated liquor caused Morgan to gasp slightly, as it overtook his sense of smell. Taking a small sip of the warm, slightly sweet liquor, he felt it trace a soothing path over his tongue and all the way down his throat.

"Ahhh!" Aunt Kitty sighed, as she swallowed a bit of her drink. Dropping her knitting on the floor, she sat back comfortably in her rocking chair, glass in hand. "Good for what bothers the spirit. So, tell me Morgan, what is really bothering your spirit? I assume that is most of the reason why you're here and not up to your own house with Alasie this evening."

"She hasn't spoken a word since we left the Simms' house today. She's just staring out the window and not saying anything."

"Don't you worry about Alasie. She'll be okay. She just needs to process everything that has happened today. Alasie knows that she is different and that people have a hard time accepting her. That was shown to her in a very hard blow today." Aunt Kitty sighed as she took another small sip of the brandy before placing the glass on the table and leaning forward as if to reveal something important. "We must also realize that grief makes us say things that we don't truly mean. Gladys knows in her heart who and what her husband was, but hearing that told to her, at that exact time was more than her mind could take in. And along with the fact that it came from someone who some people still don't know how to accept, was the tipping point for Gladys's mind to comprehend."

"I understand all that, Aunt Kitty, I really do," Morgan implored in Alasie's defence. "But what hurts the most is not that people have a hard time accepting Alasie, but the way they insult her and disrespect her. The names they call her and the way she is cursed upon is just so hurtful, when all she has done is to try to be helpful and caring to everyone. It is just not fair."

Aunt Kitty sighed and shook her head before she continued. "Life is not always fair, Morgan. Today there is a widow with six hungry mouths to feed. Yesterday she was a beaten and battered wife. Neither is fair, but which one is better? Time will see to that, not me and not you. Fair is how we look at things," Aunt Kitty spoke softly, yet firmly. "Right now, Gladys may see life as being a lot more fair to Alasie than it is to her. And I suspect that just maybe her anger is because that doesn't seem fair in her eyes."

"I see where you are going, Aunt Kitty. You are a lot smarter than we all give you credit for."

"I know, Morgan, my son," she laughed. "That's why I was given the brains in the family and your mother was given the beauty."

"What about Aunt Ruth?" inquired Morgan with a touch of humor in his voice.

"Ruth!? She got the leftovers. And believe me, they were what you would call the dregs at the very bottom of the bag." Aunt Kitty let out an uproar at her own joke.

"Aunt Kitty, you are scandalous." Morgan chuckled. "I am glad I came over."

"You come over here whenever you want my dear boy. You know the door is always open," Aunt Kitty smiled. "Oh! And make sure you tell that girl of ours that I am expecting her here after dinner tomorrow for my next lesson."

"I'll tell her, Aunt Kitty. You can be sure of that."

CHAPTER SIXTEEN

By the time Morgan reached the house he was shivering. The storm still had not blown itself out and now the temperature had dropped as the night was coming on.

Alasie had left a kerosene lamp burning low on the table for Morgan's return and had banked the stove with wood for the night. She was no longer sitting in the rocking chair, so Morgan assumed she had gone to bed. It had been a long, tiring day for them both and sleep was the only thing that would help either of them to ease the weariness from mind and body.

As Morgan climbed the stairs and headed toward the bedroom that he shared with Alasie, he paused as he reached the last step. A soft silvery-toned voice could be heard singing from further down the hallway.

Although he could not understand the words, the dulcet tone was mystical.

Walking to their bedroom door, Morgan was transfixed by the striking scene that he latched his eyes upon. Alasie sat cross-legged and unclothed on their bed, while her soft voice caressed the air in a hypnotic cadence. The radiating glow from the kerosene lantern danced to the wondrous sounds that filled the room. Shades of light and dark fondled the girl's full breasts, and her silky locks languidly brushed her dark nipples. She undulated her hands rhythmically in tune with the music, as her body swayed to and fro.

Morgan was mesmerized by the exquisite scene transforming before his eyes. The simplistic dance of arms and body held him in a bewitching trance as he stood motionless in the doorway. Continuing to sing in a lilting melody, Alasie lowered her hands as the intimacy of her fingertips traced light circles over her bared breasts in a spherical motion that continued to the roundness of her stomach. Spreading her long fingers apart, she placed them delicately underneath the slight swelling of her belly, as if holding a treasure. Alasie stopped singing and opened her eyes, glancing timidly at Morgan, who still stood silently mesmerized in the doorway.

Reaching with one hand toward him, she whispered, "Come," as she patted the bed. He placed the kerosene lamp on the bureau, walked toward the bed and sat down. Alasie reached out and taking Morgan's rough, weatherbeaten hand, she placed it next to her own on the tender flesh of her stomach.

"Alasie, are you…"

"Shhhh," Alasie whispered, raising her finger to her lips.

Both sat silent and immobile as they stared directly into each other's eyes. After a moment, what felt like a tiny shifting movement could be felt on Morgan's palm. Morgan's pale blue eyes widened with unforeseen amazement. Keeping his gaze on Alasie, whose dark eyes were sparkling with excitement, he watched as she smiled at him.

"Alasie have baby. Morgan's baby," she smiled.

Morgan grabbed Alasie in his arms, holding her close to his pounding heart, as tears of absolute joy ran down his face.

***

"I feel like a man who has been given the world," Morgan whispered into Alasie's ear as they snuggled together beneath the heavily quilted bed. "I never thought I would have a family and now I don't know how I could live without one."

Alasie let him speak his feelings, as she listened to him in silent contentment.

"A baby! Our baby!" Morgan spoke the words softly as he placed his hand once again on Alasie's stomach. "I wish Mam were alive to see this. She would be so happy," Morgan said with an edge of sadness in his voice. "Aunt Kitty will be on top of the moon about this. I know she will. You'll have to tell her when you go over there tomorrow. She's expecting you to teach her her next lesson, she told me so tonight."

"Aunt Kitty teach baby medicine too."

"Yes, you and Aunt Kitty will both be great teachers for sure."

"Not, Alasie teach, Aunt Kitty teach," Alasie said softly, with a slight sadness in her voice. "Mi'kiju, teacher. Grandmother teacher. Grandmother Aunt Kitty teach Morgan's Tu's medicine."

"Tu's?" Morgan inquired.

"Daughter."

"Daughter? Maybe it will be a son," Morgan smiled.

"No. Alasie give Morgan daughter," she said knowingly.

Morgan wasn't entirely sure he understood everything Alasie was saying but he was too excited to get into the details of what would be an unknown adventure for them all.

CHAPTER SEVENTEEN

A few evenings after Alasie's big surprise, Morgan stopped into Aunt Kitty's for a yarn and to get her reaction to the news.

Upon entering the porch, Morgan sniffed as he detected an odd odour. It was the smell of something familiar that was filling the air inside the home, but not familiar enough to allow him to pinpoint the aroma.

With his curiosity aroused, he quickly removed his boots and coat and entered the bright, cozy kitchen. Aunt Kitty was sitting at the table with her hands immersed in a pot of some sort of liquid brew that was filling the air with the mysterious smell that was playing with Morgan's nostrils.

"What in the name of God are you mixing up there?" Morgan inquired.

Aunt Kitty chuckled. "Nothing you'd want to eat, I'm sure. It's ground juniper leaves and pepper that I steeped for my rheumatism. Alasie gave me the recipe a few months ago and as God is my witness, it's working like a charm. I haven't been this free of pain in my hands for years."

"That's wonderful," Morgan smiled. "Almost as wonderful as Alasie's good news," he said as his face lit up with a grin. He had not been able to wipe it off since he found out about the baby.

Aunt Kitty lowered her eyes and sighed, wiping her hands in the tail of her apron. "I have been waiting for you to stop by, ever since Alasie told me."

"What's wrong, Aunt Kitty? Don't you think it is marvellous news?" Morgan asked, confused by the woman's seemingly nervous reaction.

Aunt Kitty rose from her chair and taking the pot, she placed the cover on the top and laid it back on the end of the stove. Morgan could see that she was biding her time and not eager to give him the answer he had been expecting. As she returned to her chair, she gave a heavy sigh.

"A baby is always a blessing, but it's just…" Aunt Kitty, who was never at a loss for words, was indeed having a hard time trying to say what was on her mind. Shaking her head, she looked directly at Morgan. "I just hope you can understand that for the good to be given, there is often a large price that is to be paid in return. I just hope that the getting is worth the giving this time."

"I am not sure what you mean, Aunt Kitty. This baby is the best thing I could ever get. I never thought about having a family until Alasie arrived and now it's all I can think about," Morgan said, almost pleading for Aunt Kitty to understand what this new life meant to him. "And once me and Alasie get married, we really will be a family."

"*No!*" Aunt Kitty immediately shouted at Morgan, shaking her head as her eyes widened in shock.

"Aunt Kitty? What's the matter? Why would you not want me and Alasie to be married?"

Morgan was dumbfounded at the reaction to what he considered to be wonderful news. Aunt Kitty leaned forward in her rocking chair towards Morgan.

"Morgan, promise me that you will never ask Alasie to marry you?"

"But Aunt Kitty, I thought you would be happy for us. For me and Alasie to stand in the church and become a real family. Whatever would make you say that we should never be married?" Morgan could not comprehend what was happening.

"Morgan," said Aunt Kitty as she reached out tenderly, to take his rough hand in her age weathered ones. "I want you to try and understand what I am saying, even though I am not fully sure I do myself. But what I do know is that if you ask Alasie to marry you, you will not get the reaction you want." Aunt Kitty's eyes filled with tears and she knew she was hurting Morgan with her words, but knew she needed to try and explain anyway. "I have spoken to Alasie and although I will not break the promise to reveal what she told me, I will tell you what I can. Alasie is not the same as me and you. Her life before she came here was not like ours. Therefore, she will never enter a church to be married and she will never commit herself to you or say the vows you want to hear. She has to do things her own way, the way she knows they have to be done, and that will not always be what we would choose. But you have to accept this, Morgan, or you will lose everything."

He was quiet for a few moments, sitting on that information. Finally, he said, his voice halting, "I won't ask you to reveal your confidence with Alasie, and I know you wouldn't do that if I did ask you."

"No, I would not. What I have told you is all I can say and for now it is all you need to know." Aunt Kitty patted the hand she had laid on top of Morgan's. Looking pitifully into his blue eyes, she saw the pain that she knew was because of her words. "Alasie loves you, Morgan. And she is so happy to be giving you a baby. A family. But do not ask her to give you more than she is able. She will not let it happen, and it will only cause you unneeded pain."

"But how do I know if what I am asking is too much or if it's wrong? How do I know what I should be doing?" Morgan pleaded.

"You have one thing to do, and it is what your mother told you the night she died. Love her, my son. Love her."

What Morgan thought would be a celebratory visit with Aunt Kitty turned out to be something bewildering. Walking back up the gravel pathway toward his home, he tried to wrap his head around what she had told him. Even though what she said was hard to contemplate, he knew somewhere in his heart that Aunt Kitty was right. As much as he loved Alasie and wanted that gift of a family, all neatly packaged and beautiful, he knew it was something that she could not give him. His family would remain different and mysterious; only revealing itself when Alasie wanted it to.

CHAPTER EIGHTEEN

December's snowfall filled yards and pathways as it drifted into sloping mounds and slanting piles. Long, silvery icicles glistened in the light as they hung like shiny, giant fingers from the eaves of brightly colored homes. And even though the days were short of warming sunlight and the nights were longer and colder, this month was always brightened by the knowledge that Christmas was about to erupt in all its lively splendor.

"I have the perfect Christmas tree," a voice came from behind the boughs of a large fir tree that filled the porch. "I just have to get it into the kitchen first."

Alasie was sitting in the rocking chair sewing, when the huge conifer sprang through the porch door filling the small entryway and started talking to her.

Morgan, poking his head between the branches, smiled at Alasie. "What do you think?"

Alasie could not help but laugh at the hilarious scene in front of her. Morgan's face was peeking through the thick branches of the large tree and looking so funny, Alasie could only giggle at what she saw.

"I know it's a bit big, but it should be okay once I get it into the kitchen," Morgan announced, withdrawing his head from between the branches, as he tried to push the overly large tree through the narrow kitchen door. "I just have to get it stood up straight, and give it a big *push!*"

And with that, the bristly fir boughs overflowed the kitchen like a bottle of bubbly champagne on New Years Eve. Morgan's push landed him on top of the tree that now lay, in all its giant splendor, across the kitchen floor. Alasie's sewing material that was on the table came flying out on her lap, while one of the kitchen chairs was shoved over by the wood box, while the kettle rattled on the stovetop as the tip of the large tree swept it as it exploded into the small room.

craned his neck at an awkward angle and saw Alasie still sitting in the rocking chair with her hands covering her mouth as she tried to hide her mirth.

"I think it might be a bit too big," he admitted, spitting needles from the tree out of his mouth. Alasie could no longer hold her amusement and doubled over as his words sent her into roars of laughter.

***

Getting the tree back out of the house proved to be quite the task as well. After chopping limbs and branches to be able to fit it through the doorways, they decided to go in a completely different direction.

"I think you may have been right about the tree being a bit too big. This little one will work just fine," Morgan grinned as he and Alasie stood admiring the top two feet of what had once been the giant monolith that Morgan had first cut down.

"Big tree toooo big. Like big monster," Alasie grinned and shook her head at Morgan. "Alasie love paper stars Morgan show her to cut."

"And the bows from all the bits of your leftover cotton really look nice." Morgan had to agree with Alasie that the lovely two-foot tree that now stood on the stand in the kitchen corner was a much better alternative to his over-enthusiastic version.

"All it needs now is this star," he said as he took a wooden star that had been painted yellow and placed it on the very top branch. "Dad made that star the same year I was born. I remember him holding me up and placing it at the very top when I was too small to reach." Morgan smiled at the thought of his life and so many treasured memories.

Alasie leaned in toward the tree, as she breathed deeply of the perfumed aroma of pine and the fresh fragrance of the earth, a bouquet that to her meant life and memories as well.

"Next Christmas, I'll be able to do the same with our baby," he smiled as he turned toward Alasie. She had wandered toward the window and Morgan could see her wipe her eyes. Morgan crossed the kitchen and wrapped his arms around her. "What are you sad about?"

Alasie looked up into Morgan's eyes. "Alasie not sad. Alasie happy for mijuwa'ji'j," she smiled, placing her hand on her swollen belly. "Morgan be good ujjl, father."

"You'll be a wonderful mother as well," said Morgan, kissing the top of Alasie's head.

Tears continued to fall down Alasie's cheeks as Morgan turned her toward him.

"Alasie, are you happy here? Are you happy about the baby?" Morgan asked.

"Alasie happy, lot happy for mijuwa'ji'j, baby. Happy for Morgan too," she smiled as she held her delicate hand against his rough whiskered cheek.

"Do you realize how much I love you Alasie?" asked Morgan gently, hugging her to himself.

Alasie pulled away and looked pleadingly at Morgan. "Morgan love mijuwa'ji'j. Not matter love for Alasie."

"What do you mean it doesn't matter if I love you or not? Of course I love you *and* I love our baby. But without you there would be no baby and so I love you so much for giving me this family that I have always wanted."

Alasie snuggled close to Morgan and whispered under her breath, "Baby be loved, most important thing."

Morgan wished that Alasie could understand how much he loved her as well as their child, but to Alasie, there was nothing more important than the baby she was carrying. She seemed obsessed that the love for this baby should mean more than anything else. Chalking it up to maternal instinct, Morgan let Alasie have her way as she loved the baby with a besotted adoration.

CHAPTER NINETEEN

Gently withdrawing from the soundness of deep sleep and with her eyes still closed to the bright light of the morning sun, Alasie clumsily pulled her hand from underneath the warmth of the thick quilts and wiped her face. Something seemed to have lightly brushed her cheek and rudely aroused the warm, peaceful comfort she had been enjoying.

Slurp!

Alasie bolted up into the bed with a look of disconcerting alarm. What felt like a soggy, wet rag had been swiped across her entire face, startling her from sleepiness to complete wakefulness in an instant.

"Ewwww, yukkk! What that?"

Yip! Whine…

Beside Alasie was what looked to be a jet-black ball of shiny fluff with two beady, black eyes poking out from inside. A flaccid, pink tongue, the soggy, wet culprit that she assumed had startled her awake, hung from the side of the animal's mouth. As it wiggled its behind in the softness of the thick quilts, she saw a quick flick of its tail before she was smothered in furry, wet dog kisses. The animal, though only a puppy, was still quite the armful as it bounced around Alasie yipping and ready to play.

"Hhhheeeeee!" squealed Alasie as the animal hopped and bounded on the bed like a rubber ball that had been let go on a set of stairs.

Reaching across the now rumpled bed, Morgan grabbed the frisky puppy. "Merry Christmas!" Morgan laughed as he handed the dog gently to Alasie. She smoothed the shiny black fur at the top of its head trying to calm it, as the animal, still wanting to play, wiggled his behind as its tongue lolled out in a winded pant.

Cradling it snuggly in her arms before it could squirm out of the restraint, Alasie started to hum softly.

"I hope you like your Christmas gift. It's a female Newfoundland dog. I knew a person from down in Francois whose dog had a new litter," said Morgan. "This little girl is all yours."

The boisterous puppy, who had by this time completely worn herself out from the stringent romp on the bed, had settled down for a nap in Alasie's arms. As she continued to hum as she stroked the smooth, silky fur on the puppy's head, tiny grunts and snores could be heard coming from the exhausted animal.

Smiling up at Morgan, Alasie whispered, "Alasie love Merry Christmas."

Morgan was relieved. He had wanted a dog ever since his mother's dog, Queen, had passed away when he was a young boy. But his mother was so devastated by the loss of her beloved companion, she did not want another animal.

Morgan could still remember the morning Queen died as if it were just yesterday.

He had been down on his father's stage head catching spiny connors and belly-web scolpins that frequented the shallow water around the wharf. His father was in the stage baiting gear for the next day's fishing.

"Save a few of those old connors for Queen, Morgan," Levi Spencer said to his son.

"I have a few right here, Dad," Morgan answered. "I know old Queen loves to chew on them."

Starting to feel a rumble in the pit of his stomach, Morgan decided to go up to the house and maybe get one of the raisin buns his mother had been baking earlier that day. He could give Queen the connors at the same time. Grabbing the stick that he had reeved through the gills of the fish, Morgan said goodbye to his father and headed up the road.

"Queen! Hey, Queen! Where are you ,girl?"

Morgan looked around as he approached the house but the dog didn't come waddling out from one of her secret sleeping spots to greet him.

Morgan remembered just a few years before, when Queen would bound joyously when her name was called. But in recent years, with age creeping into her tired old body, her joyous leaps were now solemn shuffles as she grew more and more weary.

"Hey Mam, is Queen in the house?" Morgan asked as he grabbed two of the warm buns off of the plate that was on the pantry counter. "I have a few connors for her and she didn't come when I called her."

"Morgan Levi Spencer! You dirty little bugger. Get out

of my clean kitchen with those smelly old fish," Naomi chastised her son.

"Have you seen Queen? I have these fish for her." As Morgan held up the fish, salt water and bits of blood from the dead fish dropped on the kitchen floor.

"No! I haven't seen Queen, and you need to take those fish outside. You also need to wash your hands before you eat those buns you have there."

"My hands aren't dirty. They have been in salt water all morning," said Morgan as he put the buns on the table and wiped his hand in the leg of his pants.

Naomi shook her head as she pointed her finger at the door. "Outside with those horrible smelling things," she said as she reached for a rag to wipe the floor.

Stepping outside, Morgan sniffed the fish. They didn't smell bad to him, and he was certain they wouldn't smell bad to Queen either once he found her.

Morgan peeked into the woodshed to see if Queen was taking a nap inside, but with no sign of the dog, he decided to go across to Aunt Ruth's to see if he might be over there lying on their bridge. As he turned, Morgan caught a glimpse of a brown furry tail sticking out behind the corner of the shed.

"Queen!? There you are," Morgan said. But there was no movement of Queen's fluffy tail. Stepping around the back corner of the shed, Morgan saw Queen laying on the ground as if she were sleeping, yet in the far pit of his stomach what he had felt before as hunger now felt more like fear.

Morgan dropped both the fish and the raisin buns to the ground and knelt on the ground by his old friend.

Slowly he reached out his hand and smoothed Queen's silky brown coat.

"Queen?" Morgan whispered softly. But Queen did not move, she just lay there as still as a stone.

Fear spread through Morgan like an uncontrolled wildfire. He sprang from the ground where he had been kneeling and in a voice of panic screamed for his mother.

"Mam!? Mam!?"

Naomi heard Morgan's panic and met him as he was coming up the bridge.

"Morgan! What on earth.....?"

"Mam, it's Queen. She's behind the shed and something is wrong with her! She won't move."

Naomi's face turned white as she rushed to the back of the shed.

Morgan's fear of what he knew in his heart, kept him standing by the bridge until he heard his mother's scream pierce the air.

It was then that he tore off down the road toward his father's stage.

***

Two hours later, Morgan watched heartbroken from his bedroom window as his father finally convinced his mother to leave the dog's side and come into the house. By that time a steady drizzle was falling and both Naomi and Levi were soaked to the bone. Naomi sobbed pitifully as she lay with her head on Queen's coat, smoothing the dog's head and scratching behind her ears like Queen loved Naomi to do in life.

Some time before, Aunt Ruth had come over toward

the shed to see what the communion was all about.

"Naomi, what on God's green earth are you doing lying down on the ground with your head on that dead animal?"

"Ruth, leave her alone," Levi answered. But Aunt Ruth was no easier to get along with then than she was now.

"Levi, get her up out of it. What will people think of her?"

Naomi rose her head up as she glared at Ruth. "I don't care what they think of me Ruth. I have loved this dog from the day she was born and she knows me better than most people. She showed me kindness, she showed me caring, and she showed me a damn sight more love then you are showing."

"So you think this dog loved you more than I do." Aunt Ruth stood staring at Naomi.

"I know she did," Naomi said. "I was able to count on this animal to be there with me when I needed to be comforted and to be shown love. I could also trust this beautiful animal to hold my deepest secrets, even the one concerning Morgan's birth."

"What secret about Morgan's birth?" Aunt Ruth questioned intrusively.

"Ah! You would expect me to tell you, wouldn't you, Ruth. Then you could run off and blabber your little bit of news to all the two-faced gossip mongers who you call your friends."

"Naomi, I am shocked that you think so low of me as to do that to my own sister," Aunt Ruth uttered in mock disbelief, as she placed her hand to her face.

"Don't play the righteous one with me; I know you

too well, but you will never know my and Morgan's secret because my lips will never utter it and the only other soul that knows is Queen, and she is now gone," Naomi laid her head back on Queen's coat as she sobbed. "Go home, Ruth, get away from me."

Remembering this scene that had been hiding in the far reaches of his conscience was shocking to Morgan. Why was he just realizing what his mother had said? Did having the new dog here trigger this memory? And if so, what did it all mean? What was his mother's secret that concerned him as well?

Shaking his head, Morgan knew this was not the time to try and figure out his mother's secret, but he had a strange feeling that the time would come some day soon.

As Morgan smoothed the blanket next to Alasie as he sat down next to her. His bottom had no more than touched the edge of the bed when a squeaky spring voiced its opposition from underneath the mattress. Like a lighted match to gasoline, the young dog exploded out of Alasie's arms, bouncing from one spot to another, ready for another round of frollicking fun.

***

As it turned out, to Morgan's sheer delight, the dog loved Alasie and could be found wherever she was.

"What do you think you want to name the dog?" Morgan asked a couple of days after she had been given the furry black ball of energy. "We can't keep calling her dog," Morgan laughed.

"Alasie think about name. Name important," she said. "Need name that show strength."

"So, I guess we won't be calling her Wiggles or Bounce?"

Alasie looked at him with a confused look on her face, not really understanding the humor Morgan was trying to imply.

"Alasie, name her, Oqoti (O-hgo-di)."

"Oqoti?" Morgan tried to say the word, but knew he was probably crucifying it. "What does that mean?" he asked.

"Oqoti, mean dear friend. Oqoti dear friend to Alasie."

"I think that is the perfect name," Morgan said as Alasie sat stroking Oqoti's head in her ever decreasing lap.

CHAPTER TWENTY

Morgan was angry and he had had as much as he could stand. This time Aunt Ruth was going to hear what he actually thought of her rude and contrary disposition toward Alasie.

As he marched across the yard and up the steps to the bridge, he knocked sharply on the wood door, rather than barge into the home.

He could hear Aunt Ruth hollering as she entered the porch: "If it's mummers, they won't be coming in here and tramping snow all over my floor!" As if people dressed in this Christmas tradition would even try to get into the contrary old woman's house.

Reaching for the latch, Morgan glared at his aunt. "I am not a mummer, but you still might not want to see me."

"Oh, it's you, Morgan. Why didn't you just come right in instead of getting me up out of my chair?"

"Because, Aunt Ruth, I won't be staying long and I am not here to visit." Morgan stepped back out on the bridge and pointed toward the ground of the hens' yard that was by the house. The snow-covered ground was sprinkled with bits of bannock and pink spots of the fireweed jam were sunk into the snow — the gift that Alasie had delivered just an hour before. The busy fowl were now pecking at the banished gift as if it were a feast. "Why would you throw out a gift that Alasie was gracious enough to give you?" Morgan shook his head as he awaited his aunt's reply.

As the redness rose in her face, an embarrassed Aunt Ruth sputtered as she replied, "Well, I didn't know what it was and... I... Well, I thought it was better to give it to the hens then let it dry up in the pantry."

"That is a damn lie and you know it." Morgan was mad and he wanted to at least hear the truth.

Realizing she had been caught in the lie and not liking what was happening, Aunt Ruth cocked her head up and straightened her shoulders ready to defend her reasoning. "Well, if the truth be known, I wasn't going to eat anything that girl made. Lord only knows what she mixed up in that. And that pink slop in the bottle, well, it almost turned my stomach to look at it. So I threw the devil's dirt out to the hens. I just hope it doesn't kill them." Aunt Ruth finished her tirade with a nod of her chin as if to say that her reason was understandable.

"Aunt Ruth, what has made you so mad about Alasie?" Morgan asked in a low voice. "You were never like this to me before she came into my life."

"Don't even say her name to me. That Indian you got over there didn't come into *your* life. She came and stole your mother's. She is living in Naomi's house, wearing her clothes, using her stuff and worst of all, she has fooled her son into believing she is this wonderful person."

"Aunt Ruth! Alasie has done nothing of the sort. Mam was gone before Alasie even showed up. Where do you get off saying all this about her? She has made my life so much happier and she *is* a wonderful person, but you won't give her the time of day."

"No, and I don't intend to. If you want to go on thinking she is good, then you do that, but you can tell her from me that I don't want her bringing anything else she has mauled over here to try and poison us!" Aunt Ruth was in a rage and now Morgan was getting the real truth.

"Well, I'll have you know both Peter and Daniel came over to see if Alasie had any 'flat bread and jam' left because you threw out what Alasie had given them. They're both over to the house right now with Alasie eating bannock and fireweed jelly, and loving it. When I left, Alasie, that wonderful person, was actually showing them how to make it. They want to show their mother what they're learning."

"Well, Naomi Jane can deal with that when she gets back from visiting. But there won't be anything made here that will be wasting our grub and money on foolish Indian concoctions."

Just then Gilbert, who had been sleeping off the effects of a day going from house to house in an alcoholic Christmas tradition, rose from the daybed in the kitchen. With half-opened bloodshot eyes, hair going in every direction and an overpowering stench of alcohol on his breath, he leaned on the kitchen chair to support his still drunken body. "What are you doing here, Morgan, old man."

Looking at Gilbert, he shook his head. "I am wasting

my grub and money on Indian concoctions, and not on alcohol."

Then, turning on his heel, he walked out the door.

CHAPTER TWENTY-ONE

January's snow piled and drifted on top of December's already thick, white blanket and so by the time February started her contribution, the piles had turned into rounded hills and the drifts were hulking mountains. Deep, narrow channels like battlefield trenches were cut throughout the community. Action was seen daily with an arsenal of snowballs, and battle cries from laughing children.

Morgan had been busy in his shed all morning and by lunchtime was feeling the gnaw of hunger pulling at his stomach.

"How are my women doing?" he inquired as he entered the porch, stomping his snow-covered boots on the braided mat. He dropped an armload of birch in the wood box and, removing his coat and hat, he hung them on a nail before entering the warm kitchen.

"We are both doing wonderful," Aunt Kitty answered as she stirred whatever was in the pot on the stove. "Alasie has been busy this morning," she indicated by pointing to the tiny night dresses and diapers that were displayed on the table.

"Aunt Kitty is very good teacher." Alasie smiled as she proudly held a tiny yellow nightgown against her ever-growing belly. "So happy she here with Alasie and Morgan."

Shortly after Christmas, and with all the snow that was keeping Aunt Kitty enclosed and alone in her house, Morgan suggested the older lady move into their home.

"I'm also happy that she decided to come live with us," agreed Morgan.

"Well, no one is more pleased than I am," answered Aunt Kitty, wiping the tears from her eyes with the end of her apron. "It was too hard living alone and having to fend for myself. I couldn't do it anymore."

"You don't have to worry about a thing now," Morgan said as he came over to the stove and patted her shoulder, peeking into a pot of what looked like partridge soup. "You're where you're wanted and needed. That's what counts."

Aunt Kitty, too emotional to answer, just moved toward the counter to start getting dinner set for those whom she now considered her family.

***

After they were all three seated at the table and grace was said over the scrumptious meal, conversation turned to what Morgan had been doing, causing all the beating and banging that the women had heard coming from the shed.

"Well, it's an idea that I had, and for now it's kind of a surprise. But I should have it ready in the next day or so," Morgan replied with a grin. "I also need to take Oqoti out in the shed with me after dinner."

At the sound of her name, the now sixty-pound fur-ball looked up from beside Alasie's chair where she spent most of her time. Sniffing the air and realizing there was nothing being offered to her ever-hollow stomach, she settled down for yet another snooze.

"Morgan not build house for Oqoti?" Alasie looked startled. Oqoti had spent every minute by Alasie's side since Christmas morning. She slept on the floor by Alasie's side of the bed every night and during the day lay curled up in the corner of the kitchen beside Alasie's rocking chair. The dog had become a constant companion, and she could not think of putting the dog into a house outside in the cold and snow and away from the cozy warm abode that she was now used to.

"No! I wouldn't have the heart to do that to Oqoti." Morgan glanced at the dog whose ears twitched as she lay sleeping. Probably dreaming of bouncing in the heaps of snow. "She loves to roll in the snow," he smiled, "but this is one dog that will always live in the warmth of a home," Morgan assured Alasie, who sighed with relief.

"I'm glad to hear that too," said Aunt Kitty. "That animal is like a monument in the corner beside Alasie. You never hear a word out of her unless she whines to be let outside to do her business, then it's straight back into her warm corner again."

Oqoti, as if she knew she was being talked about, sat up straight, saliva coated tongue lagging from her thick, black lips and ebony eyes staring at her beloved mistress as she drank in her fill of praise. Alasie scratched the special spot between the Oqoti's ears, where you could almost hear the dog sigh with contentment.

***

The next day, during the noon hour dinner, Morgan revealed that his surprise was now completed.

"I just need you both to dress up warmly and come outside with me so you can see it for yourselves," grinned Morgan with a sparkle of glee in his eyes.

Gulping down the remainder of his tea, he whistled for Oqoti and like a snap of a twig, the two of them were out the door to ready the surprise everyone was anxious to see.

Donning their coats and boots, as well as caps and mittens, Aunt Kitty and Alasie stepped outside into the white wonderland of snow that covered the yard.

From behind the shed, the two women could hear Morgan's voice. "Getty up! Go! Come on, you crazy dog."

Alasie and Aunt Kitty looked at each other, wondering what the commotion was all about, when suddenly from around the shed came Morgan, sitting on a chair that was attached to a sled and being pulled by Oqoti. Both women burst into gales of laughter as Oqoti pulled Morgan around the large yard on the seated sled.

"What in the name of God is that man going to come up with next," Aunt Kitty chuckled.

"That funny sled. Oqoti look happy she in the snow," laughed Alasie.

As soon as Morgan stopped the sled by the bridge, Oqoti flopped down and started rolling until her black coat was speckled white.

"So what do you think, Aunt Kitty? It should make it

easier for you to get around the harbour and visit anyone who needs your medical knowledge, don't you think?" inquired Morgan to the shocked woman.

Aunt Kitty looked at Morgan, as if his head had just fallen off. Then thinking that it was all some kind of joke, she let out a loud hoot of laughter. "Can't you just see me now on that contraption. I'd be down with my neck broken," roared Aunt Kitty.

"No, Aunt Kitty, Morgan right," said Alasie seriously. "Aunt Kitty get around, and Oqoti pull sled."

"Come on, Aunt Kitty," encouraged Morgan. "It will be fine."

Before she could object any further, Morgan had led the large woman down the steps and carefully seated her on the chair.

"Grab a hold of the handles," Morgan said. "I'll lead Oqoti so that she won't go very fast."

Picking up the reins that were attached to both the sled and the dog, Morgan whistled at Oqoti, who stood wiggling his tail ready for another round of 'pull the sleigh'.

"Ohhh! O' blessed redeemer!" Aunt Kitty shouted as the lurch of the sled runners detaching themselves from the snow jolted her.

Before long, Morgan had handed the reins to Aunt Kitty who was now being ceremoniously pulled around the yard. She looked as if she were sitting on a throned carriage, as she squealed in delight.

Aunt Ruth, who was in her house next door cutting up vegetables for the evening's supper, heard the commotion. Thinking it was youngsters playing in the snowbank by the house, she rushed out of the pantry wiping her hands in her apron.

"Naomi Jane, are those youngsters jumping in the snow by the house again? They're going to have all that snow down in the path and we'll have to shovel it out again," rattled Aunt Ruth with a contrary look on her face.

"No, Mam. That's Aunt Kitty. Come and look out at her." Naomi Jane chuckled as she turned from the window so that her mother could look through the frosted window pane.

"Tsk! Tsk! Tsk! Well, I'll be darned if she's not gone off her head all together this time," Aunt Ruth scolded. "What does she think she's doing, perched up there like hen on her eggs?"

"It's a dog sled," said Naomi Jane as she shoved her feet into her boots and bolted out the door for a better look.

"Dog sled? Look at her waving her hand, the bloody old fool," Aunt Ruth spoke out loud to herself as she too donned her winter coat and tied her bandana underneath her double chin and headed out the door.

By now, Aunt Kitty had ventured the sled out onto the road and Oqoti was gently towing her along the snowy path by the house. Spying Aunt Ruth creeping down the path, Aunt Kitty waved her hand and hollered, "Did you see me, Ruth!"

"I heard you, making enough ruckus to wake the dead," Aunt Ruth commented. "I wasn't much interested in all your foolishness. I'm busy enough that I don't have time to bother with what you are doing," she said, playing coy to Aunt Kitty's new adventure.

"Well, if you are that busy, what are you doing out here?" inquired Aunt Kitty.

"For your information, I am on my way down to the shop. We need some pork for the buns I'm going to make," answered Aunt Ruth, as she tred carefully out the path and toward the road.

"We have pork in the house, Mam," said Naomi Jane.

"Be quiet, Naomi Jane," snapped Aunt Ruth, not wanting to give away that the reason she was outside was really her complete and utter nosiness.

"Why don't you use the dog sled, to go down there?" offered Aunt Kitty, with a grin of daring on her face.

"You must have gone crazy all together. If you think I am getting on there, you got another think coming," Aunt Ruth spoke sternly, but with what Aunt Kitty knew, was curiosity in her voice.

"Yes, Mam," said Naomi Jane. "You should try it."

"Yes, Aunt Ruth. Oqoti is a great sled dog, and you'll be perfectly fine. I'll even walk down alongside you," said Morgan.

"Don't worry," Aunt Kitty fired out, with what she knew would be the winning shot. "Ruth was never as adventurous as I was when we were growing up. She was always afraid to do the fun things."

"I'll show you who can be adventurous!" Aunt Ruth hollered. "Get your big ass down off that seat and let me get up there."

As Aunt Kitty quickly slid from the seat, Aunt Ruth slid in and grabbed the reins. In a temper, she slapped the two pieces of rope hitting poor Oqoti's backside in a stinging whip. In a flash of yelps and yells, Aunt Ruth was soon tearing off down the snow-covered road like a ball shot from a cannon. Oqoti's rump stung, and she raced to get away from what she now considered a torture device. Aunt Ruth screamed bloody murder as animal and human hurtled down the road at a gallop hitting every pothole and ridge while chucking Aunt Ruth around in the seat like an exploding seed of popcorn. Morgan raced down the road after the runaway sled, while Alasie and Naomi Jane stood speechless with their hands over their mouths. Aunt Kitty, the true instigator of what could be best described as a comedy of errors, was bent to a double in an uproar of hilarity.

"Stop, Oqoti! Stop!" yelled Morgan as he tore off after them.

Morgan had nearly caught up to the sled when Oqoti had to take a quick turn in the road. Before his eyes, Morgan saw the sled tipping as Aunt Ruth, dropping the reins, went flying off the seat and into a heaping bank of snow.

By the time Morgan reached her, all that could be seen was two legs, wearing a pair of button-up, fur lined boots and topped off with the frilly ends of a pair of flour sack bloomers.

Grabbing hold of the boots, Morgan gave a huge pull, yanking Aunt Ruth out of the snowbank and onto the road.

"Are you alright?" Morgan asked as he tried to brush the snow from Aunt Ruth's face.

"Alright? I don't say I will ever be alright anymore," sputtered Aunt Ruth in a hot rage. Batting Morgan's hand away, she wiped the snow from her reddened face. Morgan was not sure if the colour was from the cold or the anger. Aunt Ruth's bandana was hanging round her neck and her normally neat hair was sticking up all over her head and beaded with bits of snow.

"Here, let me take your arm and lead you back up to the house," offered Morgan.

"I do not need anyone to lead me. I am quite capable of walking on my own two feet," announced Aunt Ruth in a heated huff, as she turned her back toward Morgan and stamped her way back toward her house. As Aunt Ruth, in a tantrum of rage and embarrassment waddled up the road, Morgan couldn't help but laugh when he noticed that her dress had become tucked into her underwear and unbeknownst to an already humiliated Aunt Ruth, she was now showing everyone the Cream of the West label on the back of her puffy white bloomers.

CHAPTER TWENTY-TWO

Morgan pulled on the mooring line that floated his dory to her place off from the wharf. He had just finished shovelling the snow that had accumulated aboard it from the night before. Oqoti, on one of the rare occasions that she left Alasie's side, had accompanied Morgan down to the wharf for a jaunt and now lay on the edge of the wharf contentedly watching the day's happenings. Tying the line securely around the post on the end of the wharf, Morgan rose to watch Gilbert who was off in the harbour aboard his boat. He seemed to be having some difficulty pulling the mooring from the water.

"Do you need any help with that mooring, Gilbert?" Morgan hollered.

Gilbert rose from where he was leaning over the edge of the bow and pointed to the bally catters that had drifted in on the southerly wind, gathering together and filling the harbour.

"The bloody ice has got my killick shifted, so I'm trying to move it back in closer to where it was before!" Gilbert yelled back to Morgan. "I just about got it there now."

Morgan held up his hand and waved to indicate that he had heard him. Leaning down, Morgan gave the line another tug to ensure everything was secure. As he rose and was about to leave the stagehead, he heard, "OOOHHH!"

Turning his head toward the sound, Morgan saw Gilbert's two legs going over the bow of the boat as he fell into the icy water.

"Gilbert!" Morgan shouted. There was no response, and Morgan could not see the man as he had fallen into the water on the back side of the dory. Morgan scrambled to untie the mooring line that he had just secured. He knew he only had minutes to try and get aboard his boat and get to Gilbert before the bone chilling water got him.

"Woof!" Morgan looked up just in time to see Oqoti sailing off the end of the wharf and plunging into the frigid water.

"Oqoti!" Morgan screamed at the dog. But she was already paddling towards the boat from where Gilbert had fallen.

Morgan rushed to finish pulling in the dory and climbed down the wooden rails of the stagehead. Looking out to the empty boat in the harbour, he could see neither the dog nor Gilbert. Frantic with worry, Morgan hurriedly untied the oars that were secured against the wind and was about to put them between the tholepins when he spied Oqoti. She was towing Gilbert through the water with the collar of his jacket in her mouth as she headed for the shore.

"What's going on?" shouted a voice from one of the other wharves.

"It's Gilbert, he fell overboard off of his boat!" Morgan yelled frantically as he looked up and saw several other men on the road by his stage watching the happenings like a staged play.

Realizing that the dog would be able to pull Gilbert to shore before he could get to him, Morgan raced back up the railings and down toward the landwash below the stage.

"My dog has him in tow. Everybody come down to the landwash and we'll get him from there," Morgan instructed.

The men gathered at the shoreline just as Oqoti came close to the shore. With the water wading off to the top of their rubbers, they grabbed Gilbert from the freezing water and up the rocky incline to the road as fast as possible.

Oqoti shook herself to rid the icy water from her thick coat and raced knowingly to the sled that was on the road by the stage. The men lifted a freezing, wet and unmoving Gilbert to the sled as Morgan placed the harness over Oqoti's large body. One of the men sat in the seat of the sled holding Gilbert, as Oqoti barrelled up the road toward the warmth of the man's home.

Morgan wasn't sure if Gilbert was still alive. There was a nasty cut on his forehead and blood streamed down his face along with the icy salt water.

Before the sled that was carrying Gilbert reached the house, someone had gone on ahead and informed both Aunt Kitty and Alasie who were now waiting frantically for them to bring the injured man.

The women had moved the table from the middle of

the kitchen and made space for the men to bring Gilbert into the warmth of the home.

"Lay him on the floor on this quilt," Aunt Kitty directed the men.

Alasie got down on the floor alongside Gilbert and promptly ripped apart his jacket and shirt. Placing her head to his wet chest, she tried to listen for a heartbeat, but with everyone in the kitchen moving about and the cries from both Naomi Jane and Aunt Ruth, Alasie could not hear a thing.

"ALL PEOPLE LEAVE!"

Lifting her head from Gilbert's chest and manifesting a voice that demanded authority, Alasie had no sooner given the command than everyone was gone out the door. Naomi Jane, Aunt Kitty and Morgan stood in total silence by the window holding their breath as Alasie once again lowered her head to listen for what would mean life or death.

Thump... Thump... Thump. A faint but beating heart could be heard coming from inside Gilbert's broad chest.

"He alive!" Alasie gave a sigh of relief. "But heartbeat small," she indicated by holding up her thumb and finger that were just slightly separated. Grabbing a pair of scissors from the table, she started to cut off the icy wet clothes from Gilbert's body.

"Oh, thank God," Aunt Kitty let out the breath that she had been holding. At least her son was still alive. "Ruth, go get some more blankets and Naomi Jane, you get the beach rocks in the oven to warm them up. We have to put them around his body to try and get his temperature up," Aunt Kitty ordered, as she pointed to each of the women.

Morgan and Alasie removed Gilbert's wet clothing and, with the help of one of the men who was still outside the house, they lifted Gilbert onto the daybed. Morgan and Alasie rubbed Gilbert's chest and limbs furiously as they tried to get the blood circulating throughout his ice-cold body.

"Give me some of those beach rocks, Naomi Jane," Morgan said. "They should be warmed up now."

"Rocks warm Gilbert, but Naomi Jane need warm Gilbert too," Alasie said, looking at the man's wife. "Naomi Jane take off clothes. Get on bed with Gilbert. Skin and skin, warm him quicker."

Standing in the middle of the kitchen, Naomi Jane boldly stripped down to her birthday suit.

"Naomi Jane!" blared Aunt Ruth, turning away from her naked daughter in complete embarrassment. "In the name of God, have some decency!"

"Shut up, Mom! I am trying to save my husband's life," Naomi Jane stated authoritatively at her mother. Climbing on the couch beside her husband, she snuggled close to him in a loving attempt to bring him back from the brink of an icy death.

Morgan laid the warmed, round rocks close to Gilbert's body as Aunt Kitty and Alasie piled on the quilts and tucked them around the husband and wife.

"That cut on Gilbert's forehead needs to be looked at too," Aunt Kitty said, using a cloth to wipe away the blood that had run down the side of Gilbert's face.

"He must have struck his head on the boat or on a piece of ice that was in the water when he fell," Morgan said. "There was nothing else around that he could have hit his head on."

"Alasie, I think you should do the same with Gilbert's head as you did with Peter's leg. Pack it with a paste of bunch leaves and cover it with Balsam Fir sap," Aunt Kitty declared. "It worked wonderfully for Peter. It should work for Gilbert too. I'll clean it with vinegar first, to make sure there is no dirt in the cut."

Alasie nodded, as she poked through the flour sack medicine bag for the medicinal supplies she would need.

"Why hasn't he woken up yet?" Naomi Jane inquired, snuggling close to her husband, as she prayed to God that the heat from her body would be enough to warm him and bring him back to her.

"I don't know for sure, but I suspect that the smack on the head has more to do with his not coming around than the cold," his mother replied, with sincere concern in her voice. "For now, all we can do is wait and pray."

It was after Gilbert's head was bandaged, and everything that could be done was taken care of, that Alasie remembered her dog. She had not seen Oqoti since early that day when she had left the house with Morgan.

"Where Oqoti?" she inquired of Morgan.

"I had Peter let her into our house when we got back," Morgan answered. "She was soaking wet and cold from her swim and so Peter took off her reins and let her into the house."

"Alasie go see Oqoti," she said, rising with more effort than usual from the chair.

Morgan could see that the day's physical and mental strain, as well as her being in the late stages of her pregnancy, had taken its toll on Alasie. Until now he hadn't realized just how exhausted she looked.

"You stay right there in that chair. I will go and get Oqoti and bring her over here. The fire is most likely gone out in the stove by this time, so I would say our heroic pup will be only too happy to curl up by the warm stove over here," Morgan smiled as he left to go get the dog.

"That big mutt will have black hair all over my clean kitchen if Morgan brings it over here," Aunt Ruth muttered.

"*It* is a *she,* and *she* just saved your son-in-law's life. You should be grateful to Oqoti instead of squawking like a broody hen," Aunt Kitty snapped at her stubborn sister.

"Umph!" Aunt Ruth sounded like a disgruntled pig as she turned her back to everyone and headed up the stairs.

"Ruth, my maid. You would test the patience of Job."

***

Early that evening and with Morgan's insistence, Alasie finally gave in to her tired body and allowed him to lead her laboriously up the stairway to one of the bedrooms. But not before she had Morgan make her a promise. "You come get Alasie if Gilbert wake, right?"

"I promise you if you go to bed now, I *will* come and get you if there is any change in Gilbert at all."

As a fatigued Alasie departed for the night, and without a word from anyone to the contrary, Oqoti followed behind her mistress, where she too would be settling down for a well-deserved rest.

"I hope Oqoti jumps in bed with Ruth," Aunt Kitty laughed, watching the Newfoundland dog lumbering up over the stairs.

"Aunt Kitty," Naomi Jane reprimanded the older lady. "That would give Mom a heart attack, and we have enough to deal with tonight with Gilbert."

"Yes, I know. But honest to my God, Naomi Jane, I don't know how you are able to put up with your mother. She may be my sister, and perhaps I will go to hell for saying this, but her face is like a hen's ass. It's screwed up from daylight to dark."

"I know Mom seems contrary, Aunt Kitty, but what you don't realize is how much she is still grieving Aunt Naomi's passing. I have never seen her cry as much as she does since she died. Most evenings she is sitting here in the kitchen knitting with the tears rolling down her face. When you ask her what's wrong, she talks about things that she and Naomi did together."

"We all miss Naomi. She was the glue that held us together as sisters, but we can't be mad with everyone else because the Lord decided it was Naomi's time."

"Mom is still hurting, and you know what Mom is like. If she is upset about something, then she thinks everybody should be upset. That's just her way. Sure, she would be the same thing if the Lord had taken you."

"Well, I can tell you right now, and I'd tell Ruth if she was here too. When I die, don't go snotting and bawling over me. I'd rather for everyone to throw a party and say, 'Wouldn't Kitty have the time if she was alive tonight.'"

"Oh, Aunt Kitty, you are one of a kind."

CHAPTER TWENTY-THREE

As midnight approached, and with there still being no change in their silent, unmoving patient, Morgan suggested that the women go to bed. "There is no need for all of us to be breaking our rest," Morgan said. "I'll stay up and keep the fire going and if Gilbert wakes, I will let you know."

"I have to move and go make my water, but I am not going to bed," Naomi Jane replied. She was still wrapped tightly against her husband. "I'll stay up with Morgan. I won't be able to sleep anyway, so I am just as well off here."

Aunt Kitty pushed her hand inside the quilts to feel Gilbert's body. "He feels warm to the touch now, so I don't see any reason for you to stay tucked in by him anymore."

Morgan wandered outside to provide Naomi Jane some modicum of privacy to get redressed, as Aunt Kitty removed the tightly wrapped quilts from both Gilbert and his wife.

Returning from the bridge and rubbing his hands together as he stood by the stove, Morgan looked down at a deathly still Gilbert.

"I thought Gilbert would be awake by this time. What are your thoughts on it, Aunt Kitty? Is there anything else we can do?"

"I wish I knew something that could be done, but I don't. I feel useless when there is nothing to do, only wait."

"Wait and pray, Aunt Kitty."

"Yes Morgan, my son. Just wait and pray."

***

"It's six o'clock. The sun will soon be rising," Morgan said as he looked out of the kitchen window.

"Looks like it's going to be a beautiful day." Naomi Jane rose from the chair to stretch her stiff limbs.

It had been a long night and Gilbert was still not moving.

"Morgan, I want you to know that I am so happy for you and Alasie. I have grown to love her and I can't wait to see your new baby."

Morgan turned from the window and smiled at Naomi Jane. "I'm glad to hear you say that. I know you'll do everything you can for Alasie and our baby. I don't think I have been happier in my life. I just wish everyone would accept her like you do."

"I think you would be surprised at how many people here want to accept her, but I suppose they just don't know how to go about it. She is a lot different from Aunt Kitty, who they are used to, but I have a feeling that change is coming."

"Ahhhhh," Gilbert moaned as his head turned slightly on the pillow.

"He's moving!" Naomi Jane cried, as she knelt on the floor by the daybed where Gilbert had been lying since the accident. "Gilbert? Can you hear me?" his wife pleaded, as she caressed his cheek.

"I'll go and wake up Aunt Kitty and Alasie," Morgan said as he ran up the stairs.

Within minutes, the kitchen was a humbug of activity as everyone was up and gathering around to see the miracle they had all prayed for come true.

"How are you feeling, my boy?" Aunt Kitty inquired as she leaned down by her son.

"Head hurts," Gilbert mumbled almost incoherently. He weakly raised his hand and covered his eyes.

Alasie sat on the bed beside Gilbert and gently pulled his eyelids apart. The intrusive light made Gilbert wince, as it flooded his eyes. The pupils of both eyes were large enough that very little of his hazel-green irises could be seen.

Aunt Kitty who had been peering over Alasie's shoulder, saw this as well.

"Big eyes from hitting head. He going to have hurting head for some days," Alasie explained. "Need to move him to bed and make room dark. Light hurt Gilbert."

"Of course we can get him up to bed. Daniel, can you help Morgan get your father up the stairs?" Naomi Jane asked her son.

"Yes, Mom. Morgan and I can get him up there," Daniel replied, only to glad to be doing something to help.

Alasie put her hand on Daniel's shoulder. "Need to be

careful. Your father be dizzy." Daniel nodded.

Sitting on the side of the daybed, Morgan spoke softly to Gilbert. "Gilbert? Can you hear me?"

Weakly raising his hand, he grunted in acknowledgement.

"Me and your boy are going to take you upstairs and make you more comfortable. I'm going to sit you up now," Morgan explained to him as he slid his arm underneath Gilbert's shoulders to raise him from the pillow. Then he gently turned Gilbert's legs and put his feet on the floor, keeping a tight hold on a very unstable Gilbert as he sat up on the couch.

"Daniel, you get on the other side of your father and put your arm around him. I'l tell you when to lift him," Morgan told Gilbert's fifteen-year-old son.

Daniel, doing as he was instructed, sat beside his father and positioned his long arm behind his father's broad back. Gilbert turned toward his son and opened his eyes in a reflection of total confusion. "Who are you?" he asked quietly, looking into his son's face.

"Dad, it's me. Daniel," he said looking even more confused than his father. Gilbert closed his eyes and looked away. Daniel's eyes filled with tears. The realization of his father not recognizing him was like a smack in the gut.

"That normal after hitting head. He know you soon," Alasie said. She had seen Daniel's shocked reaction upon hearing his father's words. Understanding his pain, she laid her gentle hand on his shoulder to reassure him, as well as the rest of the bewildered family.

Daniel and Morgan soon had Gilbert up on unsteady feet. They slowly moved him upstairs to spend what would be the remainder of his recovery, in the comfort of his bed.

While Gilbert was being tended to upstairs, Alasie had slipped outside, returning shortly with several alder branches that she had plucked from the trees that were numerous around the community.

"Tell me now, my girl," Aunt Kitty asked. "What do you intend to do with alder branches that will help my son?"

"Alasie peel off bark and scrape off what inside it."

Aunt Kitty watched as she saw the supple white inner bark being scrapped into a small pile on the table.

"Alasie need small bowl, peppermint, and long cloth."

Aunt Kitty, knowing where to retrieve the required items, soon had them in front of Alasie. Putting the inner birch shavings into the bowl, Alasie went to the boiling kettle and poured in a small bit of hot water to soften the shavings into a paste. Mashing the mixture together, she then let several drops of the aromatic peppermint fall onto the paste. The fragrant smell soon overpowered the kitchen as Alasie transferred the paste to the long cloth.

"This need be wrapped on Gilbert's head every day. Do this for bad pain in head."

"Let's go upstairs and get it done, so that we can try to get some relief for that poor boy of mine."

As Aunt Kitty and Alasie reached the top of the stairs, Aunt Ruth was coming out of the bedroom with a blanket in her arms.

"Gilbert just threw up all over the bed and the floor," she said, passing Aunt Ruth and Alasie as she hurried down over the steps with the soiled quilt.

Rushing into the room, Naomi Jane was wiping Gilbert's pale face with a wet rag. "Now he's sick and just threw up!" Naomi Jane cried frantically as the two women entered the bedroom.

"That okay. Gilbert sick because he move around. He still have very bad head."

"We have a bandage here that Alasie made for the headache Gilbert has. We'll put it on now and it needs to be changed every day until his head is no longer hurting."

"It smells like peppermint," Naomi Jane said.

"It does have peppermint in it. Now Alasie, what else do you think will help Gilbert get back on his feet?"

"Dark room. Sleep. Quiet house. Make sure drink, steep partridge berry in water and drink two times morning and supper. Not eat lot. Little, like soup."

"Okay, let see," Naomi Jane said. "Make the room dark." She hurried over and pulled down the green blind, shutting out the sunlight that was flooding the outdoors with its brilliance. Then returning to the side of the bed, she continued, "The bandage needs to be changed every day. You will do that, right?" she inquired of Alasie.

Alasie nodded.

"I have to steep a few partridgeberries and get Gilbert to drink it, like a tea, twice a day. He shouldn't eat a lot at a time and soup would be good. I think I got it."

Aunt Kitty smiled and put her arm around Naomi Jane's shoulder. "You will be fine, my darling girl, and we are only across the yard if you need anything."

Tears streamed down Naomi Jane's face and she suddenly looked haggard from the mental toll that she had been experiencing for the last day. Sitting on the bed beside her injured husband, she finally let out the anguish that had been building up inside her as she sobbed piteously.

"Why don't you lie down alongside Gilbert and have a nap too. You've been up all night," Aunt Kitty suggested, as she hugged Naomi Jane in her arms, wiping her tears and kissing her on her still damp cheek.

"I think I will; I'm too tired to do anything else right now anyway."

Aunt Kitty and Alasie left the room, closing the door behind them to give the battle worn couple some quiet and comfort.

Naomi Jane stripped down to her underclothes and climbed under the heavy, warm quilts to, once again, snuggle next to her husband.

Reaching out to touch his cheek, she whispered into his ear. "I love you, Gilbert."

"I love you, Naomi Jane," came a soft reply.

CHAPTER TWENTY-FOUR

After the initial medical care that Alasie had given to Gilbert, the remainder of the bedside attention was passed over to Aunt Kitty. Alasie did not want to tempt Gilbert into yet another rage toward her like he had previously done and so passed any further care on to his mother.

"I haven't heard Gilbert say a word against you, Alasie. I think he's just glad to be feeling better," Aunt Kitty assured her.

"That good. But Alasie not go to house. Not want cause anger."

Understanding Alasie's reasoning, for the next week while Gilbert rested in bed, his mother tended to his nursing needs.

***

"Come in and shake the snow from your coat, old girl," Aunt Kitty spoke to Oqoti as they both entered the porch after their ride back from a neighbourly outing.

"Did Aunt Kitty have good visit with friend?"

"Yes, indeed I did. Eliza told me to tell you that her

cough has been getting better ever since you sent her the Aster flowers to steep out. Along with the goose grease she has been rubbing on her chest and the bottoms of her feet, she should be right as rain before you know it. She said to send her thanks and she made several bands to wrap around the cord on your baby's belly when she comes."

"That so nice but Alasie not ask for anything. Only want to help people."

"Just accept the gift as thanks for what you are doing. People around here don't have much, but what they do have, they share. They use these offerings to say thank you when things are done for them and to not take them is almost like an insult. It's like saying what they are giving you is not good enough."

Alasie nodded in understanding.

"Now, speaking of things done for people, I have a surprise for you. When I was down to Eliza's today, her granddaughter Beatrice stopped by. She and a few other young women want to stop by and see you."

"See Alasie! Why see me?"

"Well, they want to meet you and welcome you to the community. It's about time, I say. But I suppose it's better late than never. They also have some things they want to ask you concerning your knowledge of medicine."

Alasie looked at Aunt Kitty with a stunned expression.

"The best part is, after what you did to help Gilbert, their men are encouraging them to come here and make you feel welcome in Cape La Hune. Isn't that wonderful? They want you here to stay," Aunt Kitty clapped her hands together as she beamed with delight. "I think they'll be here tomorrow afternoon," Aunt Kitty said, as she busied herself around the kitchen.

Alasie turned her head toward the window and stared across the bay as a tear trickled from her eye.

***

"Is there anyone home?" a voice called out from the porch.

"Yes, we are home, come on in," Aunt Kitty cheerfully greeted four young women, as they entered the porch. "Hang your jackets wherever you can find a place and come in. I just got a pot of tea steeped, and a pan of buns taken out of the oven."

"It smells wonderful in here," one of the women replied. She was tall and a bit on the skinny side with curly brown hair. Alasie, who was sitting in her usual place by the window, knew she had seen each of the women before but did not know their names or anything about them.

"My name is Beatrice, by the way," she said to Alasie. "I hope you don't mind us dropping in like this, Miss Alasie."

Alasie recognized the name to be Eliza's granddaughter that had approached Aunt Kitty about this gathering.

"Not Miss. I Alasie," she smiled at the young woman. "I glad you come to Alasie's house."

"Well, I think it is about time we made you feel welcome, Alasie," said another woman. "My name is Joan and these two are Mildred and Lydia," Joan pointed to the women standing around the kitchen.

"Now make yourselves comfortable and I am going to get a cup of tea for everybody," Aunty Kitty announced as she started to take the cups and saucers from the pantry shelf.

"No tea for me, Aunt Kitty. I have been getting heartburn so bad lately. Especially when I drink tea," Lydia piped up. "But I will have a glass of water."

"Alasie can give you something for heartburn that will fix you up in no time. Can't you, Alasie?" Aunt Kitty grinned.

Alasie knew what tricks Aunt Kitty was up to. Getting Alasie talking and showing her medicinal skills. She smiled at the cunning old woman, before turning back to the curious women seated around her table.

"Fireweed," she said as she looked at Lydia. "Steep fireweed in pot and drink like tea."

"But what's fireweed?" Lydia asked unknowingly.

"Isn't that the long purple flowers that grow up by the cemetery every year?" Mildred asked.

"Yes, that's the ones," Aunt Kitty nodded.

"Lord save me," Lydia laughed. "I had them in a bottle on my table all summer and didn't even realize it was something that could have helped me."

Alasie got up, went to the hook behind the door and took down her now, well known, medicine bag. Reaching inside, she withdrew a small, dried animal skin pouch she had sewed from the skin of the rabbits that Morgan had caught earlier that fall.

"Alasie have dried fireweed but fresh better," she told Lydia as she removed a handful of the dried flower stems and handed them to the woman. "Steep four in cup of water. Drink when you feel burn. Next summer you find fresh and use two."

"Thank you so much, Alasie," Lydia smiled.

"Do you want me to make a cup for you now?" Aunt Kitty asked.

"Well, if it's not too much trouble, I would love one."

"Alasie, I have to admit, when you first came here, I was a bit unsure about you and what you were doing. Well, if truth be told, I was more than a bit unsure," Beatrice admitted to Alasie as the other women all nodded in agreement.

"Alasie understand. She different and people not know who Alasie was."

"Do you mind if I ask who taught you so much about medicine?" Mildred asked.

Aunt Kitty turned toward Alasie, trying to gauge her reaction to the question asked of her in total innocence. She knew that Alasie's life before coming to Cape La Hune was something very personal and private, something she rarely spoke about. Aunt Kitty also knew, from what Alasie had revealed to her in confidence, that this community was not ready for Alasie's truth to be told.

Alasie, nodded knowingly at Aunt Kitty's worried reaction to the question that had been posed to her. "Alasie's Mi'kiju, Grandmother teach Alasie. She Sagaligesw in Alasie's tribe," she answered with a smile.

"What does that word mean?" Joan asked "Sagal….."

"Plant Woman. Plant medicine so Mi'kiju Medicine Woman."

"So what you are saying is that your grandmother was the medicine woman in your tribe and that she taught you how to use medicine like she did," Lydia inquired after hearing Alasie's revelation.

"Yes, grandmothers teachers for granddaughters."

"Well, that's not much different than what our grandmothers do with us, now is it?" Mildred looked questioningly at the other women. "Most of our mothers were busy raising a family, so it was our grandmothers who taught us to knit and sew, and I suppose if they knew anything about medicine they would have taught us that as well."

"Joan, do you remember the day when we both got our monthly for the first time," Beatrice asked her twin sister. "We had just turned eleven only a few months before and still stunned as sticks. We both thought we were dying and ran to Mom crying. And what did Mom do? Sent us over to Grandmother Eliza for her to deal with us and she was the one that explained what was happening."

"I remember only too well. I was sure I was dying and I said every prayer I knew between our house and grandmothers," Beatrice laughed. "And there are still a good many months when I feel like I am dying, when those blasted cramps come around. It's bad enough we women have to go through having monthly's and babies but to have the pain is wicked in times."

Alasie smiled as she reached, yet again, into her medicine bag, like a magician pulling out a rabbit from a bag of tricks. "This help with monthly pain; it Cramp Bark and it need be boiled in water. Just small piece and help pain. Help for backache in your men too."

"Well, I'll be. You are a real miracle worker." Beatrice smiled.

"Alasie not miracle worker. That Kji-Niskam, Great Spirit. He create world and make medicine to help people."

"So is your Great Spirit like our God?" Lydia asked. Alasie nodded.

"Speaking of God, I guess you have done a lot of thanking him for saving Gilbert," Mildred said, turning to Aunt Kitty.

"Indeed I have and I have done a lot of thanking Alasie as well. I am sure that Gilbert would not be here or not be as good as he is if not for what Alasie did for him. She saved his life along with Oqoti here, they gave me back my son."

"I believe you, Aunt Kitty," Joan piped up. "My Eli was down there when it happened, and he said he didn't think there was any chance Gilbert would come out of it. He said that dog was amazing and the strength she had to swim off and to pull Gilbert out of the freezing water was something you almost had to see to believe."

Alasie was feeling embarrassed over the oohs and awws from the women as she tried to put an end to the praise she felt was unnecessary. "Gilbert good now. That what matters."

"You are way too modest, Alasie. You did a great thing and even the men are amazed that Gilbert is up and around, good as new. And you can believe me, it takes something pretty big to get a compliment from some of them." Mildred rolled her eyes.

Alasie blushed from all the praise and even though she felt shy from all the attention, she understood that this is what it took for her to achieve the acceptance she so desired for herself, but mainly for her baby.

"I'd say we should be on our way, don't you think, ladies?" Rising from the table, Joan took her cup and saucer to the counter.

"Yes, we don't want to overstay our welcome."

"Oh, you don't have to worry about that Lydia. Does she, Alasie?"

"No, Alasie love having you, Joan, Lydia, Mildred, Beatrice. Alasie happy you come see Aunt Kitty and me."

"Well, I suppose before too much longer we will be coming to see the new baby."

"Yes please! Come see daughter."

"Daughter or son?"

"Alasie has been insisting it is a girl ever since she's been carrying it. And you know, I think she is going to be right," Aunt Kitty laughed.

When the women had all said their goodbyes and thank you's for the tea and medicine that they took with them, Aunt Kitty let out a sigh of relief.

"Well, that went wonderful. Did you enjoy the day with the women, Alasie? They seem to have really appreciated the help you gave them."

"Alasie enjoy day. Now baby be accepted by people. That all that matters."

CHAPTER TWENTY-FIVE

There was much lively chatter around the supper table that night as both Aunt Kitty and Alasie told Morgan about their visitors.

"It was a wonderful day, Morgan. The women all yarned and Alasie gave them some of the wonderful stuff from her medicine bag for them to use for this and that. It was wonderful, just wonderful," Aunt Kitty said so happily that tears ran down her chubby face.

Morgan laughed as he turned to Alasie. "From what Aunt Kitty is saying, I think you girls had a 'wonderful' time."

Alasie laughed. "Yes. Mildred. Joan. Lydia. And... Beatrice. Were ladies." Alasie wanted to remember their names as she felt it showed a sense of sincerity for each of the women. "They talk to Alasie and Alasie help them. Give them medicine."

"But did you enjoy having them here?" Morgan posed the question he was hoping to have answered.

"Alasie enjoy women. Now they accept Morgan's baby."

"But they also accept *you*," Aunt Kitty stressed, trying to make Alasie understand that she was the focal point in this new adoption of trust.

"You need to listen to Aunt Kitty. You are very important too. You are this baby's mother, and you are the woman I love and that makes you just as important as our baby."

As Aunt Kitty rambled on not noticing the change in Alasie's demeanor, Morgan watched as Alasie closed her eyes and her jaw stiffened, while her knuckles turned white, as she squeezed her fists tightly. He realized too late that he and Aunt Kitty had pushed Alasie too far this time and she could stand it no longer. "Baby *most* important. Aunt Kitty, Morgan need understand. Alasie want *baby* accepted. Alasie not matter. *Alasie not matter!*"

The usually timid woman yelled loudly at Morgan and Aunt Kitty as she jumped from the table and headed for the stairway. Too emotionally agitated to realize what was around her, Alasie came face to face with Gilbert who had been standing in the kitchen doorway.

With her mind in such a distressed state, Alasie's thoughts immediately flashed back to the night Gilbert had previously filled the same doorway in the drunken tirade against her care of his son.

With her mind spinning in a mass of perplexity, Alasie's legs softened as the floor reached up to grab her. A chilling scream exploded from her throat as she felt Gilbert's hands grab her body. The touch of hands on her body unlocked horrific images within Alasie, that travelled from dark hidden cavities to the open doorway of her mind.

Then everything went black.

***

Morgan held Alasie as she sobbed frantically. "Alasie not want hurt baby. Not want hurt Morgan and Aunt Kitty."

"Don't worry, my love. You didn't hurt anyone. You just got yourself too worked up and you fainted. All of us, including the baby, are fine. But you need to rest. That was Aunt Kitty's orders before she went back downstairs."

"Alasie get too angry. But Morgan know Alasie want best for our daughter. She so important. Alasie need Morgan understand."

"I do understand. And our baby will be loved, and she will be cared for, and she will have the best that I can give her. But I want you to understand that as long as you are with me and I am able, you Alasie, my sweetest love will also have the best of me."

Alasie gave Morgan a tender smile as she snuggled deep into the feather mattress and closed her eyes.

Waiting until he heard the cadence of her breathing steady to an even rhythm, Morgan then eased himself from the bedside and ventured back downstairs.

Aunt Kitty and Gilbert were both sitting in the kitchen chatting in a hushed whisper when Morgan entered the room.

"How is she now, Morgan?" Aunt Kitty got up and wrapped her arms around Morgan. "I have never been so frightened in my life. I thought for sure our girl was gone."

"She's doing better and she just drifted off to sleep."

"I am sure seeing me in the door did not help her any. I know she thought I was here like I was the last time, to let all hell break loose."

"I'm sure that's probably the straw that broke the camel's back, Gilbert old boy, but you weren't the thing that started it. Alasie has been fixated with this baby and wants everyone here to be good to him or her once they're born. I know she hasn't been treated very well until lately, but this need to see the baby be taken care of has become an obsession for Alasie."

"Well, I didn't help matters when I came here after she helped Peter. I don't know what I thought she was going to do to anyone but for some stupid reason, I didn't trust her. I think it was because she was different, but that should never be a reason to show the hate I did towards her.

"Well, I say you should have got that smack on the head long ago if that's what it took to change your attitude," Aunt Kitty said. "And if I knew that's what it took, I'd have knocked your poor, old father over the head when we got married and maybe he wouldn't have been so stubborn before he died," Aunt Kitty spit out, shaking her head.

"That's why I came over here. To thank Alasie for saving my life and to tell both of you how sorry I am for coming here and blaring at you like a crazy man after what she did for my Peter."

Gilbert reached behind his chair and lifted up a tiny white cradle and placed it on the table. "I wanted to give this to Alasie as a thanks for all she did for me and my family."

Morgan ran his hand over the smooth railing of the tiny cradle that he knew would brighten Alasie's face when she saw it.

"Why don't you come over again tomorrow and give it to Alasie yourself. I know she will be so happy with the gift, and I'll warn her before you arrive this time," Morgan laughed.

"Make sure you do. I don't want anyone else fainting when they see me." Gilbert chuckled. "Oh, and by the way. If you ever decide to breed your dog, I would like one of her pups. That dog was strong enough to tow my large frame through the freezing water from two-hundred yards? I still can't believe it yet."

"Well, I would advise you that if you ever get a dog, make sure Ruth is dead and buried or there will never be any peace in your house again."

Gilbert let out a guffaw as he headed out the door.

CHAPTER TWENTY-SIX

Aunt Kitty had just gotten her breakfast finished when she heard the sound of footsteps coming down over the stairs.

"Good morning, Aunt Kitty. Would you mind coming up and seeing Alasie? She says she isn't feeling very well this morning and asked me to come and get her medicine bag. To tell you the truth, she doesn't look good at all."

"Yes, you know I will," she said as the two hurried up to the bedroom where Alasie had been since the evening before.

As soon as Aunt Kitty saw her, she knew something was wrong and had a good idea what was happening. "Oh! My darling girl, you are swelled up like a pudding." Alasie's face was puffy and there was a dark shadowing underneath her eyes. Aunt Kitty knew that fluid was being retained inside her very pregnant body. "Show me your legs," she said, as she peeled back the blankets from over Alasie's body. Her legs were nearly twice their normal size, and the skin was swollen tight. "Just what I thought: you're keeping in all your fluid and it's making you swell."

"Head hurts too."

"Yes, and you need to stay in that bed while I take care of you." Aunt Kitty turned to face Morgan and instructed, "I need you to go outside and get some alder branches. We need to do a poultice for Alasie like she did for Gilbert."

Morgan fled from the bedroom to get the alder that grew out in the backyard.

"Alasie, what do you think is best for the swelling? I can get it ready if you tell me."

Reaching into the bag, Alasie pulled out a small pouch and handed it to Aunt Kitty. "This Wisowtaqjijl (Goldthread). Steep small bit in water for Alasie. Need steep partridgeberries too. Help Alasie make water more. Take away inside water."

"Okay, my dear. You rest here," Aunt Kitty said as she pulled the quilt back over Alasie. "I'll go and get everything ready before I come back."

"Pull down blind please, Alasie's head hurt bad."

Aunt Kitty crossed the bedroom to the window and pulled down the dark green blind, casting Alasie in darkness while the sun was shining brightly over Cape La Hune.

***

Morgan was at the table scraping the inside of the alder bark into a small pile when Aunt Kitty came into the kitchen looking more than a little worried.

"Alasie is not well, is she, Aunt Kitty? Tell me your honest opinion."

"I have seen this before when women have been pregnant, especially just before the baby is due, and everything has still been fine. But I am worried. Alasie seems like she is very weak and very swollen. This is not good, as a woman will require all her strength when she goes into labour."

"Hopefully we have a bit of time yet to try and get Alasie back on her feet before the baby comes."

Shaking her head, Aunt Kitty sighed. "I don't think we have as much time as we were hoping. That baby has dropped and I expect Alasie could go into labour at any time."

"What about the baby? Is it too soon?" Morgan choked the words from his throat, that was now as dry as sandpaper.

"I think the baby is far enough along, but my concern is if Alasie will have the strength to go through the labour like she is feeling now."

"I can't lose Alasie, Aunt Kitty. She means too much to me."

"Yes, I know Morgan, but Alasie can't lose this baby or you might as well kill her now. That baby is Alasie's whole reason for living and I am afraid if the baby doesn't make it, neither will the girl we both love."

CHAPTER TWENTY-SEVEN

"Did she eat any of the soup I sent up?" Aunt Kitty questioned Morgan as he came down the stairs and into the kitchen where he placed Alasie's, still full, bowl on the counter.

His face was haggard as he shook his head, unable to get out a word. Placing both hands on the counter, his shoulders sagged and he sobbed. "She doesn't have the strength to sit for more than a few minutes. When I tried to get her to eat something, everything made her sick to her stomach. Even the smell makes her gag. She drank the cup of Goldthread tea, but she hasn't eaten now for the past three days."

"I know, Morgan, my son. She is not well and I am just as concerned as you. If only the swelling would go down. Her body is as tight as a barrel with all the water she has built up inside. I can't help but wonder what we have to face when the baby decides to come."

A thump in the porch indicated visitors, as Gilbert and Naomi Jane came into the kitchen.

"How is everybody doing today? Any change in

Alasie?" Naomi Jane asked, with concern in her voice.

"Nothing so far, and she still can't get anything down."

"I know this isn't a good time for visitors," Gilbert said, "but Naomi Jane and I really wanted to see her. I still wanted to show her the cradle I made for the baby."

"She's not up for a long visit but you are both family and I am sure she would love to see you." Morgan forced a smile that just as quickly waned from his face. "Why don't you both go on up. She was awake when I left her a few minutes ago."

"We won't stay long," Gilbert nodded as he took the tiny white cradle in his arms and mounted the stairs behind his wife.

***

"Are you up to a couple of visitors, Alasie?" Naomi Jane asked as she rapped on the door and entered the semi-dark bedroom. A lantern was lit on the table by the bed and its low light cast an eerie shadow pattern on the bedroom walls. The floor creaked as Naomi Jane walked slowly toward the bed. She tried not to show her shocked expression to the young woman laying there helpless and vulnerable, but was sure she had not done a very good job. Could this actually be the same young woman who days before looked healthy and beautiful in her pregnancy? It was almost impossible to believe that one person could look so different in such a short amount of time. Alasie's face was bloated and her hair hung limp and dull. Dark circles etched her swollen eyes and made them appear as dark slits cut into the flesh, while the sparkle that always brightened her face was lost to the unruly anguish that was now seeking hungerly to steal her beautiful spirit.

Noami Jane slowly lowered herself to sit on the edge of Alasie's bed and reached out for her swollen hand. Tears rolled down Alasie's face as she looked at the woman who was like a sister to her. "Alasie, love Naomi Jane. You good friend to Alasie."

Naomi Jane tried to tell Alasie the same but choked on the words. Reaching down into the bed, she hugged Alasie and kissed her cheek, before she stood and walked slowly back to the bedroom door. There was so much that she wanted to say but after seeing Alasie she could not get the words out past the lump that had formed in her throat. Naomi Jane's heart was breaking apart within her chest as she watched Gilbert walk his gruelling road to forgiveness.

"I made this gift for the baby," Gilbert whispered as he placed the cradle on the floor by the bed so that Alasie could see it.

Alasie smiled weakly. "Beautiful bed for Alasie's beautiful daughter. Thank you, Gilbert."

Gilbert's large frame shook as he stared at the stricken face in the bed. Feeling as if his legs would not hold him, he knelt on the hard floor beside the bed and leaned closer to Alasie. Whispering softly, Gilbert poured out the pain and anguish that had been squeezing his heart since his accident: "I am so sorry, so very, very sorry for how I have treated you. I don't know how I could have thought you would do anything against any of us. You are much too good and I was much too ignorant." Gilbert put his head down on the bed and wept silently. "You could have let me die after how I treated you. But you didn't. You cared for me. Your heart is so much better than mine."

Extending out her hand, Alasie gently laid it on Gilbert's shoulder. "Alasie not angry at Gilbert. Gilbert look out for his family, that all. Gilbert be good man now."

Raising his head and looking directly at Alasie, Gilbert nodded, as repentance in the form of tears, rolled down his face. Guiding Alasie's swollen hand to his lips, Gilbert placed a kiss on the tender flesh. "Goodbye, Alasie," he whispered in a voice that only she heard.

"Gilbert forgiven," she whispered back.

***

As the distraught couple came down the stairs, Morgan stood rigidly in the doorway of the kitchen. Naomi Jane glanced at Morgan as streaks marked her face from the tears that flowed like rivers from her eyes. Unable to utter a word, she pulled the latch on the door and rushed outside where sounds of agonizing sobs could be heard as she ran across the yard. Gilbert understood his wife's heart-rending need to escape and as much as he wanted to do the same, he hesitatingly pulled in a deep breath and forced himself to move toward his tortured friend. Morgan stood like a man frozen in time as Gilbert laid a heavy hand on his heavy, stooped shoulder. Then, raising his head, Morgan and Gilbert looked at each other seeing remorse reflected in the other's face.

Gilbert turned and walked out the door in silence.

CHAPTER TWENTY-EIGHT

Aunt Kitty sighed heavily as she looked up the long narrow stairway. She carried two cups of tea in her arthritic hands, one for herself and one that she hoped would serve as a lifesaving remedy for both Alasie and her unborn child.

Alasie was failing fast, and Aunt Kitty knew that before too much longer no tea, nor anything, would be able to save them.

Alasie had become like the daughter Aunt Kitty never had, and to watch her slowly fading was breaking her heart into a million pieces. Yet, pushing forward up each of the thirteen stairs, Aunt Kitty tightened the grip on her emotions as she reached the bedroom and entered with a cheery greeting of, "How is our girl feeling on this beautiful sunny afternoon?"

"Alasie tell baby she come soon."

"Yes, that's right. That baby needs to make herself known so that we can get you well again." Aunt Kitty forced a smile. She knew it was a very big question as to whether mother or baby could even survive the whole birthing process, yet she wouldn't let on to Alasie what she feared.

"I have a cup of tea for you and me both and I am going to sit with you for a while."

"Where Morgan?"

"I finally got him to leave the house for a while. Gilbert was going down to the landwash to get some kelp to put in the garden and I told Morgan he should go and get some for us. Oqoti took off with him. I guess she was feeling cooped up too." Aunt Kitty helped Alasie sit up in bed to drink her tea, piling the pillows behind her back and making her as comfortable as she could.

Seizing the opportunity given her, Alasie knew Aunt Kitty would come to understand what she was about to do, and why. Alasie had taken a huge risk months before, when she had revealed her true self to Aunt Kitty. Although Alasie knew it was hard for the woman to realize the immensity of what she had been told, she also knew that this woman, her friend, mother figure and confidant understood enough. She also knew that Alasie had no choices in life and no way out of what she had to do.

"Alasie feel hunger. Aunt Kitty get Alasie small piece bread please?" Alasie inquired, knowing that Aunt Kitty would do whatever the girl needed, if she thought it would help her feel better.

"Oh, I certainly will. Finally, you may be coming around. I will be right back," Aunt Kitty said as she rushed out the door as fast as her heft would allow.

Alasie listened for Aunt Kitty to start slowly down the stairs before reaching for the white medicine bag that was laying on the table by her bedside. Finding the dried skin pouch she needed, she carefully opened it and extracted a grey-brown powder. Taking a small pinch between her fingers she reached across to Aunt Kitty's teacup, sprinkling the substance into the liquid and mixing it with her finger to ensure it was completely dissolved before the woman returned.

Replacing the pouch inside the medicine bag, Alasie placed it back on the bedside table and sat back against the pillows as she awaited Aunt Kitty's footsteps on the stairs.

CHAPTER TWENTY-NINE

"Morgan? Morgan?" Naomi Jane screamed as she ran down the road toward the landwash where Morgan and Gilbert were gathering kelp that had washed up onto the shoreline.

Gilbert rose from his bent position as he heard the frantic hollering. "That's Naomi Jane's voice. Somethings wrong!" he said to Morgan who was standing just a few feet away.

Morgan's face paled as he scrambled over the slippery kelp covered rocks, trying to get to the road above. Oqoti, who had been splashing along the water's edge, barrelled over the rocks toward the two men.

By the time both men and dog were over the ridge and onto the pathway, Naomi Jane had reached them.

"What is it? What's wrong?" Gilbert shouted as he looked at his disheveled wife. Her face was tear streaked, and she gasped for breath from the strain of running all the way down the road.

Wiping her nose in the sleeve of her dress, Naomi Jane looked at Morgan and choked out a reply, "It's Alasie!

Aunt Kitty said she's gone!"

As Morgan and Oqoti raced up the road toward the house, Gilbert and Naomi Jane hurried along behind them. "Did Aunt Kitty say that Alasie was dead?" Gilbert gasped.

"No, but she must be. Aunt Kitty was in the upstairs bedroom window hollering for help when I heard her. She said to go and tell Morgan that Alasie was gone."

"That doesn't sound like Mom at all, to be screaming out of the window," Gilbert choked out as he and Naomi Jane raced toward the house.

Morgan had already reached the house and was racing up the stairway taking multiple steps with each stride. His mind was in such turmoil that he hadn't had time to prepare himself for what he was about to encounter inside the bedroom. But the incomprehensible scene that met him face to face, was nothing that his mind would have ever perceived as possible, had he even tried.

***

A dishevelled Aunt Kitty was slouched on the floor beneath the open window as she tried to hold herself upright with her arm straining on the floor beside her. A colourful mat that was always neatly laid by the bed was tangled and partly under one of her legs. From her leg ran a small stream of blood that was pooling in a dark stain on the braided rug, while a blue china cup lay in shattered pieces beside the bedside table.

Oqoti, who had clambered up the steps behind Morgan, sat beside the bed with her head resting on the mattress and let out a long mournful whine.

That's when Morgan realized that the bed where Alasie lay only hours before was now empty.

"Where is she?" Morgan asked looking from the bed to Aunt Kitty. "Where's Alasie?"

"She's gone, Morgan. Alasie is gone!" Aunt Kitty cried.

Gilbert and his wife had just reached the bedroom and heard the revelation from Aunt Kitty. Naomi Jane ran over to where the older lady was slumped on the floor.

"Help me get her up and onto the bed," she motioned to the two men who were standing in complete confusion. Lifting the heavy woman, they guided her to the bed as a bright red trail of smeared blood followed them across the white painted floorboards. Naomi Jane grabbed a towel that was hanging on a nearby washstand and kneeling on the floor beside her, pressed it firmly to Aunt Kitty's leg to try and staunch the blood flow.

"Aunt Kitty, please tell me where Alasie is?" Morgan knelt down so that he was face to face with her.

"I don't know where she went, Morgan. All I know is that she left here."

"But she was too sick to leave! She was dying, Aunt Kitty! How could she have left?"

"Morgan. Sit down and listen to me. Alasie must have put something in my tea because all I can recall is sitting here by her bed and then feeling very strange. It was like the room was spinning and full of bright lights and colours. I tried to move but my body was like I was glued into the chair and I couldn't utter a word. I was starting to get frightened," Aunt Kitty said, reaching out her hand and rubbing the pillow where Alasie had laid, "but that's when I saw it."

"What did you see, Aunt Kitty?" Naomi Jane asked.

"I saw a light. It came down from the ceiling and covered Alasie. She was glowing. The light was like it went into her and she shone like the sun." Aunt Kitty looked at Morgan. "It was beautiful and warm and all I could feel was love. That's when Alasie got up from the bed, as beautiful as the first time I saw her. She leaned down by my chair and kissed my cheek, but I couldn't move or speak. But she knew what I was thinking because her last words to me were, 'I love you too.'"

"You must have been seeing things, Aunt Kitty," Morgan said gently.

"No! I am sure of what I saw and I know it was real because Alasie told me enough a few months ago for me to know that what happened today was how it had to be. Like I told you before, Morgan, Alasie was not like us. She was here because she was meant to be, but her life was not really her own. What I just saw and what you will see before this day is done will seem unbelievable, but will be real." Aunt Kitty insisted. "If it wasn't real, then you explain to me where Alasie is now. Because she is certainly not here."

CHAPTER THIRTY

"We have to look for her!" Morgan shouted as he raced down the stairs.

"Do go with him Gilbert," Naomi Jane insisted. "I will stay here with Aunt Kitty."

"Yes, Gilbert. Keep an eye on Morgan because this is liable to kill him. He loved her more than anything and he won't give up until he finds her or he dies trying," Aunt Kitty said, with a sound of grief in her shaky voice.

***

Gilbert found Morgan outside in the shed as he searched the property for Alasie.

"Gilbert, I have to find her. She can't have gone far. She wasn't well enough to get anywhere other than around this area," Morgan said frantically, as he peered behind the shed. His eyes were bolting from their sockets, and he looked like a man possessed.

"I'll go and check in our house," said Gilbert, not knowing where else to look.

"You do that, and I'll go to a few houses down the

road."

Gilbert was just about to go into the house when Peter turned into the yard on his way back from being down the road.

"Hey, Dad! Is everything okay? I just saw Morgan running down the road and you look like you've seen a ghost."

"It's Alasie. She's gone and we can't find her anywhere."

"Alasie? I saw her about a half-hour ago," Peter replied.

Gilbert raced down from the bridge and roughly gripped his son by the shoulders. Looking into his face in sheer panic, he shouted, "Where is she? Where did you see her?"

"Geez, Dad, calm down! Alasie is fine." Peter was shocked at his father's startling reaction.

Letting go of the tight grip on his boy's shoulders, Gilbert failed to settle the panic that was in his voice. "You don't understand, Peter. Alasie is not fine. She's dying."

Peter's look of bewilderment at his father's statement which definitely did not coincide with the Alasie he had seen and spoken with just a short time before.

"Stay right here and don't move; I have to go and get Morgan."

Gilbert raced down the road to where Morgan was desperately searching for the woman he loved.

"Morgan?! Morgan?!" Gilbert yelled as he reached one of the houses where Oqoti was sitting in wait outside the door.

"Gilbert!" Morgan shot from the door of a neighbouring home. "Have you found her?" he questioned in a panicked tone.

"I haven't, but Peter saw her only a little while ago. Come on, he's up by the house waiting for us."

Both men raced toward the yard where Peter was standing. He was feeling bewildered by all the commotion that was taking place around him and why everyone was in a panic about Alasie.

"Peter, where is she? Where did you see Alasie?" Morgan gasped, as he rushed into the yard.

"I'm not sure where she is right now. She didn't say where she was going when she got into the boat."

"Boat? What was Alasie doing in a boat?"

"I think we should go inside so that Peter can tell us the whole story," Gilbert said, as he placed a hand on Morgan's shoulder to guide him towards the house.

"I don't have time to be sitting down and chatting!" Morgan shouted. "I need to find Alasie now!"

"Peter, start from the beginning, where did you see Alasie?" Gilbert asked in a calm voice, trying to ease the tension while making some sense of what they were hearing.

"I was over on the inside beach when Alasie just showed up. She asked me if I could put off one of the rowboats that were hauled up there, so I put off our little blue one."

"Did she say why she wanted to go out in the boat or where she was going?" Morgan asked, in a voice that was a shade less panicked, but much more confused.

"No, but I asked her if she needed me to go with her and she said that she had to do something on her own. Then she put her hand on my cheek and told me to always keep my kind heart."

Morgan's face paled. "Peter, how did she look? Did she seem sick or weak?"

"Not that I noticed," Peter said, shaking his head. "But now that you mentioned it, she seemed different. She looked like she sparkled, like a light was shining not on her but through her." Peter shook his head. "Never mind what I said. It doesn't even make sense."

"It makes more sense than you know, my boy," Gilbert whispered, as he looked at Morgan.

"Gilbert, where is your storm lantern?" Morgan asked.

"It's in the shed. Peter, can you go and get it for me, and make sure it's full of kerosene?"

Morgan ran into the house and came back carrying the blanket that had previously covered the daybed in the kitchen. Reaching into the open door of the shed, he took down an oil coat from the nail on the wall and a sail bag, that had once belonged to his father. Stuffing the oil coat and the blanket inside, Morgan slung it over his shoulder. Meeting him in the yard, Peter handed Morgan the battered, red storm lantern.

"Where do you think she is, Morgan? I assume you are going to look for her."

"I think I know where she is, but I don't know what to expect when I get there," Morgan said as his eyes stared across the bay towards Dead Man's Cove.

"Do you want me to go with you?" Gilbert asked, knowing the answer before Morgan uttered a word.

"No, Gilbert. Whatever happens, don't come looking for me. You need to stay here with your family and I need to go find mine."

CHAPTER THIRTY-ONE

Each splash of the oars brought Morgan closer to his hope of finding an answer to what was happening. He also knew that whatever he found would very likely change his life forever.

His mind raced back to the night his mother died, how she tried to tell him about Alasie before she drew her last breath. To his dream about the bones. Was Alasie the snow-white skeleton? Was the baby held within the body, his baby that Alasie now carried? None of it made any sense.

Morgan knew that if this is what he now had to face, then he too would die with them. He would make sure of it. He knew he could not, and did not want to live, if his family were no longer with him.

Shaking his head, to try and rid himself of the images that were taking over his mind, Morgan heaved harder on the oars. Oqoti stood with her large front paws on the bow of the boat, striking a majestic pose like a figurehead on a sailing ship.

"We will soon be there, old girl," Morgan said to Oqoti, who turned her shaggy head toward him and whined as if telling her master to hurry.

***

The sun was sinking below the western hills of Cape La Hune Bay as Morgan's rowboat slid over the smooth rocks on the shore of Dead Man's Cove. The small blue boat that had been used by Alasie was barely stuck to the shore and the stern was starting to swing in the rising tide. Morgan tied both boats to some slanted tuckamore trees that were deeply rooted just above the high tide mark.

Oqoti, who had leaped ashore as soon as the boat touched land, was sniffing her way along the shoreline. Morgan was sure she was following Alasie's tracks. Grabbing up the sail bag from the bottom of the boat, he swung it over his shoulder as he grabbed the storm lantern with the other hand. Glancing up and seeing that Oqoti was stalking the rocky shoreline with her nose to the ground, Morgan followed where the big Newfoundland dog was leading as she searched for her mistress.

"Alasie! Alasie!? Where are you?" Morgan hollered as he stepped up and down over large boulders that lined the shore. Walking a little further, Oqoti suddenly stopped in her tracks. As her head bolted up from the ground where she had been sniffing, her floppy ears stood more erect. Sticking her nose in the air and sniffing, she turned in a complete circle as if to find out the direction of the strongest scent or sound that she had detected. Suddenly Oqoti was bounding through the thick fir trees and tangled alder branches that covered an area on one side of the small cove, just above the landwash.

"Oqoti! Oqoti?" Morgan called frantically to the dog. What had she heard or smelt? Morgan was certain it had been Alasie, but now the dog was gone as well.

Morgan stopped and looked at the tangle of thick trees and matted undergrowth where Oqoti had seemingly disappeared only moments before. Knowing how hard it was going to be for him to get through the intertwined boughs, especially with the sail bag over his shoulder, Morgan knew he was better to go above them and over a ridge that was further up the side of the cove, but away from the wooded snarl.

Morgan's progress was slow as the mossy ground was soft and spongy from the recent snow melt. The berry bushes were still in their dormancy, but they tangled in his legs and feet as he tried to get through them and up toward the rocky ridge.

Rising one leg upon a small rock that was in his chosen path, Morgan rested his arms across his knee as he took a minute to catch his breath. Looking toward the ridge that was only a short distance from him, Morgan was just about to set off again when he heard a loud, whining cry coming from above him and near the ridge where he had been heading. The cry sounded as if it were from someone hurt or sick. Morgan's adrenaline shot up as Alasie's face became the picture in his mind.

"Alasie! Alasie? Answer me. Where are you?" Morgan was gasping for breath, as he half-ran, half-crawled over the remaining distance to the top of the ridge.

Once there, Morgan stopped and looked around. Not hearing anything, he called again: "Alasie! Please, where are you?" Morgan's head started to slump, as desperation started to suck the adrenaline from his exhausted body.

Suddenly there it was again! The same whining cry filled his ears, only this time it was closer and sounded like it was coming from below the ridge. Morgan scrambled clumsily down a steep rocky incline on the side of the ridge, scraping his hands as he slid roughly down the scree. On a stony outcropping, below the ridge, lay Oqoti. She was stretched out on the rough ground on her stomach, as an agonizing cry came from the animal and filled the air. Oqoti did not move, even as Morgan approached, but instead just lay staring at a small opening in the rocks as she whined piteously.

Morgan dropped the sail bag beside the dog and moved toward the gap in the rocks.

There was no movement or sound coming from inside the cave. Yet, Morgan knew as he squeezed through the entrance that he would never come out the same, if he even came out at all.

CHAPTER THIRTY-TWO

Stepping inside the cave, the dank, smell of earth and rotting vegetation overwhelmed Morgan's nostrils as the darkness claimed his eyesight. As compensation for his losses, Morgan's other senses heightened to where he could hear the waves splash on the shoreline below, taste the thick stench of decay and mold on his tongue, and feel the unlevel terrain underneath his feet.

Reaching into the pocket of his pants for a pack of matches, Morgan knelt down and felt for a place on the floor, level enough to rest the storm lantern.

"Morgan."

It was Alasie's voice. Morgan was sure of it.

"Alasie? Where are you?"

As Morgan scrabbled to light the lantern and see Alasie's face, he dropped the matchbox he had been holding as he heard the matches scatter across the rocky floor of the cave. "Damn!" In a panic, he was feeling all around the cold, wet floor when something softly brushed his shoulder.

"Morgan, there is no need."

Glancing up from where he knelt on the hard, wet ground, Morgan was transfixed as the cave started to glow. A brilliant stream of shimmering white light extended down from the rock covered roof and its luminosity filled the interior like a warm blanket. Standing within the light was Alasie. She smiled at Morgan as she lifted her hand upward, signalling for him to rise.

"Alasie? You're feeling okay." Morgan gasped, as he rose from the floor. So overwhelmed to see her, he stepped forward, holding out his arms to encircle her close to him.

"No, Morgan!" Alasie put up her hand and stepped back from Morgan's embrace. "I am perfectly well, but not in a way you would understand."

Feeling complete confusion at her rejection, Morgan tried to contemplate what was going on. That was when he was stricken with the changes that he had not realized upon first seeing Alasie.

Standing erect in the soft glow that encompassed her, Alasie was clothed in a stunning regalia of Indigenous attire. Her knee-length dress, along with her small slipper-like boots, were made of a tanned animal hide and adorned with shells and beads. Her long hair hung down her back in a smooth, silky braid while a leather strap entwined with feathers was affixed to the front and trailed down by the side of her high cheekbone.

She looked like the pictures Morgan had seen in books from the schoolhouse that he had attended as a child.

"Morgan, I want you to know my life and my story. I want you to understand why I needed you and how I unexpectedly fell in love with you." Alasie spoke softly as she smiled at Morgan.

"Alasie, you no longer have an accent," Morgan replied.

Laughing with a twinkle in her voice, Alasie answered, "Nothing is the same here, Morgan."

"But I don't understand, where is here?"

"That is something for you to find out, but not for many more years. For now, you are needed here in this world, as you have a wonderful life to live."

"But Alasie, my life will not be worth living if you are not with me," he implored.

"What you do not realize, Morgan, is that I have not 'lived' for the last two hundred years. What you also need to know is that if not for your mother, I would never have been at peace."

"So you did know my mother," he gasped at the shock of now knowing that his quiet belief was real.

"I did not know your mother, but our souls connected in a chance circumstance, and we were both given our most priceless wishes."

"Given by whom?"

"Another question you must wait upon," Alasie smiled.

"Then can you tell me where my mother met you?"

"Morgan? Don't you understand? She met me here in this cave, just like you did."

Morgan's mouth suddenly went as dry as sand, as he began to piece things together.

"Both you and your mother saw me here in this very cave. You, the night she died and your mother the day you were conceived." Alasie stepped to the side as the light shone on the skeletal remains laying on the ledge in the back of the cave.

"That is me, Morgan. That is where I spent the last days of my life and where my daughter died within me."

"No, Alasie. No. That can't be you," Morgan cried out in pure agony. "I know it's not you because I have held you and kissed you and loved you with everything in me. You're here now with me," he demanded. "How can you say that some old bones are the woman I love?"

"Because it is true. Morgan, I died over two hundred years ago, and I died a death that was hate-filled and cruel. I was taken by force from my home in a land we called Mi'kma'ki. I was taken by cruel men that killed my husband and my people. They took me aboard a large ship where I was locked in a room and treated worse than an animal. We sailed for many, many days, and as each day passed, I was beaten, raped and starved."

Morgan fell on his knees by the ledge as he painfully listened to Alasie's words.

"After weeks at sea, we became caught in a storm and the boat was taken into this bay for shelter. Later that evening the captain came to the room, but this time, I was ready for him. I had torn a large piece of wood from the bunk and as he came into the room I struck him across the head. I don't know if I killed him, and I really didn't care. I just needed to get away."

"How could you possibly have gotten away, Alasie?"

"I made my way to the aft deck and I jumped. I jumped into the water and I swam. We were not a long way from shore and I had always been a strong swimmer, but this time it was different. This time, the water was so cold, as it was late in the fall. But more importantly, I was about to have a baby. You see, Morgan, I was heavily pregnant when I swam ashore and found this cave and I was in labour when I climbed up on this ledge and froze to death with my unborn child still within my womb."

"Oh, Alasie," he moaned. "How could someone do these things to you? How could someone hurt you so much?"

"Morgan, get up and look at me." Alasie spoke softly as Morgan rose to his feet and turned to face her.

"I will soon have to leave you, and because of you I can now be at peace."

"What about me, Alasie? What about my peace?" Morgan pleaded, as tears rolled down his face.

Alasie smiled. "You will have peace Morgan. And joy and love and so much of life's wonders will fill your days. You will always carry our love in your heart and you will grieve me too, but it will be worth the price you have paid. I wanted you to know my story because I want you to teach people that the evil that happened to me has to stop. This kind of hatred cannot go on and love is the true answer."

Morgan stood grief stricken as he stared at Alasie. "If love is the answer, then why are those that I love being taken away from me?"

"I was never yours to start with Morgan, but I know you love me and I love you too. That's why I chose your mother as the one who would carry a baby who would one day become the father of my daughter. The daughter who died in my womb before she had a chance to live. The daughter who has so much to bring to this world and who needed to be born to prove that love can conquer all."

Alasie looked down in her arms and holding them forward she placed love in the crook of Morgan's arm. Love in the form of an innocent child, love in the form of his daughter and Alasie's daughter. A baby created of pure love.

EPILOGUE
SEPTEMBER, 1962

Alice Catherine Spencer gripped the iron railing of the steamer as she watched the familiar coastline passing before her. The gentle September breeze caused a few of her black silky locks to loosen from the stylish braid she had entwined together that morning in front of the mirror. The pale blue coat that she wore matched perfectly with her eyes that were the same shade as her father's.

A hand rested gently on her shoulder but she didn't have to look to know it was her father, Morgan.

"Will you miss this land, Dad?"

"I'm sure I will, my sweet girl. But it is time to go."

"Yes, there is really not much left in Cape La Hune for you, is there?"

"There is nothing left now that you are going away," Morgan sighed.

Alice was the only reason why Morgan was still alive, but she was more than reason enough. She had been his joy and his true reason for life. She gave him so many wonderful moments that he never had a chance to feel empty. Alice was Morgan's world.

"Dad, you could always come to Halifax with me. We could get a place together."

Morgan raised his hand to stop the plea that he had heard so many times before since Alice had received the letter from Dalhousie's Faculty of Medicine accepting her into the university in Halifax, Nova Scotia.

"No, my girl. You need to live your own life now. You don't need your old dad tagging along behind you and getting in your way."

"Dad! You know you wouldn't be in my way. I would love to have you with me."

"Well, if I went with you then who would make sure the Newfie Bullet made it across the island on time?" Morgan laughed.

"I suppose you're right," Alice chuckled. "I'm so happy you got the conductor job. It will keep you busy, and you won't have time to think about me."

"My darling girl, I will be thinking of you every minute from the time you leave until I see you again."

"Well, don't worry about me then. I will be fine."

"I know you will because you have your mother's determination and willpower. And like her, you will be a great Medicine Woman."

"I am proud to be her daughter, Dad. Even though I didn't get to meet her, you and Aunt Kitty have made sure that I knew who she was."

"She made Aunt Kitty promise to teach you what she had taught to her. She had so much caring and love in her heart for others but her greatest love was always you."

"I believe Mom knows that I am doing what she always wanted for me. There are times when I feel her close to me. It's like a soft voice inside of me, and it edges me forward when I start to doubt myself. Does that even sound believable, Dad?"

As Morgan looked lovingly at his beautiful daughter, he felt the caress of a small, warm hand slipping gently into his and saw a soft glow brushing his shoulder and he knew she was with him.

"Remember to always believe in the unbelievable because one day it may just change your life forever."

THE END

ABOUT THE AUTHOR

Kimberly Durnford-Courtney is originally from the isolated community of Francois, on Newfoundland's southern coast.

She many years owned a tour company with her husband Charles that did boat and hiking tours of several resettled communities around the area. She has always fostered a love of the stories, culture and history of the area she called home.

She spent twenty years in municipal politics and was chairperson for the Local Service District of Francois.

She currently lives in Hermitage, Newfoundland.

Dead Man's Cove is her first novel.